‘I have c

Alisa stare … d
astonishment … d.
She had neve…

‘Unless it’s a request to shoot you in the foot, forget it! Do you seriously think that after last night I would do more than watch with interest if you were floating downstream in a sinking canoe?’

By some superb self-control Luc kept his temper, and looked down at her with intent dark eyes.

‘It has become very obvious that last night I spoke too hastily,’ he admitted coolly. ‘I did not know then what I know now. We are in need of your services, *señorita*, and I hope you will not refuse.’

‘What services?’ Alisa demanded angrily. ‘You pointed out last night how utterly incapable I am. How have I improved overnight?’

‘You have stopped being deceitful for one thing,’ he stated icily. ‘You are no longer wearing that ridiculous disguise!’

Patricia Wilson was born in Yorkshire and lived there until she married and had four children. She loves travelling and has lived in Singapore, Africa and Spain. She had always wanted to be a writer but a growing family and career as a teacher left her with little time to pursue her interest. With the encouragement of her family she gave up teaching in order to concentrate on writing and her other interests of music and painting.

Recent titles by the same author:

NEVER A STRANGER
COMING HOME

AN INNOCENT CHARADE

BY

PATRICIA WILSON

MILLS & BOON

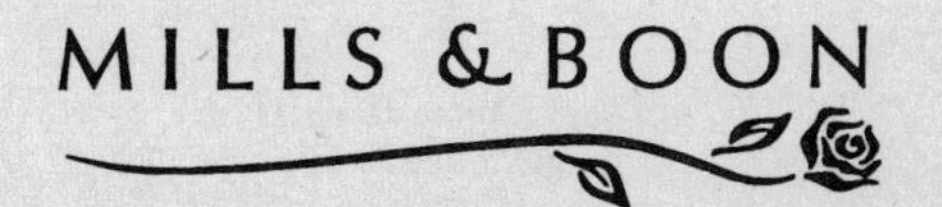

All the characters in this book have no existence outside the imagination of the author, and have no relation whatsoever to anyone bearing the same name or names. They are not even distantly inspired by any individual known or unknown to the author, and all the incidents are pure invention.

MILLS & BOON and the Rose Device
are trademarks of the publisher.
Harlequin Mills & Boon Limited,
Eton House, 18-24 Paradise Road, Richmond, Surrey TW9 1SR

ISBN 0 263 79610 8

Set in Times Roman 10 on 11½ pt.
02-9609-56132 C1

Made and printed in Great Britain

CHAPTER ONE

ALISA was just taking off her shirt when Douglas Ellis burst into her room.

'Guess what?' he exclaimed as Alisa hastily pulled the shirt around her and glared at him, her blue eyes brilliant with annoyance.

'I've guessed. You've forgotten that this is my room!' She gave him a further burst of blue-eyed annihilation. 'You spend so much time here that you've lost track of your own room.'

'Listen,' he urged, ignoring everything. 'This is real news, and anything else is of no importance. The prof is off on an expedition.' He looked at her in a very superior manner. 'Of course you didn't know that, did you?'

Alisa's expression changed from annoyance to watchful anxiety, and she turned her back, sliding into her shirt and quickly doing up the buttons. By now the blue eyes were worried, and she turned to Douglas as she tucked the checked shirt back into her jeans.

'You'd better tell me all about it,' she ordered seriously. 'If he's keeping it from me, then it's something dangerous.' She frowned and shook her head. 'He can't be going. He would have told me. Things like that take months to organise, and he just could not have kept it to himself for that length of time. Uncle Bill is incapable of holding his tongue.'

'It's true, Al,' Douglas informed her emphatically. 'He's posted up a notice. I've been trying to corner him all morning, but you know what he's like. Getting him after his lecture seemed to be a good idea, but right in the middle of it he suddenly looked up into the air, snapped his fingers and walked out. That was the last we saw of him.'

Alisa didn't doubt it. Professor William Fenton was very eccentric and given to quite bizarre behaviour—often looking at friends as if he didn't know them, sometimes tackling strangers with enthusiastic affection, as if they were long-lost dear ones. Had it not been for his brilliance, he would have been asked to retire ages ago. Everyone knew it. His students adored him and covered up for his lapses without hesitation. Alisa knew without any misgivings that nobody would even whisper about the professor's lapse this morning.

She adored him most of all, though, and knew him best. Professor William Fenton was her Uncle Bill and he had brought her up almost single-handedly, with the odd bit of help from his housekeeper Betsy. Now Alisa often felt that she was bringing *him* up, and he was very tricky to handle.

Not that it was senility. Uncle Bill was as sharp as he had ever been, but as she had grown older he had seen no reason to cling to convention any longer. He had relapsed into his peculiar ways simply because they suited him best. The trouble was that they didn't suit the world at large. At sixty, he was healthy, rotund and vigorous, with a brilliant academic career behind him. He was an authority on the civilisations of South America, fascinating to listen to, his papers awaited with reverence all over the world.

If something else occurred to him, however, he would pursue it and abandon whatever he was doing at the time. That was the worry. In the old halls of the university he was safe. Out in the wilds he was not safe at all, and

Alisa bit harder at her lip as she stared at Douglas worriedly.

'I've got to stop him, you know,' she stated earnestly. 'He'll fall off a cliff, drown in a lake or do something worse that I haven't even thought of yet. Where is he going?' she added, sitting down and pointing to another seat for Douglas.

'Bolivia. Up into the Andes. Leaves in two weeks.'

Douglas seemed to think it was amusing, but Alisa jumped up and looked at him in horror.

'Bolivia! He's not! I can't allow it!'

'Al! Your Uncle Bill might just be the cleverest chap in the world,' he laughed. 'Why do you treat him as if he's a moron?'

'Because he's not safe to be let out,' Alisa informed him heatedly. 'Not even on a clear day. He may be the cleverest chap in the world but he can't cope with ordinary life.'

'Let him be,' Douglas urged in amusement. 'Stop being the mother hen.'

'I can't let him be because something will happen to him, and I love him too much to ignore the possibility.'

'Well, there's nothing you can do,' Douglas stated flatly. 'The expedition is all fixed—the date, the place, the lot.'

Alisa paced about, frowning, worrying and thinking, as Douglas watched her with ironic eyes. She was a brilliant medical student and he knew that she had only come here to keep an eye on her uncle. She had had offers from every university she had applied to. And she was tough. She should have been living away from the university during her last year, but she had managed to get a room here to be near the prof, and he wouldn't have been at all surprised to discover that she had given somebody a mental battering to get the room.

'I'll have to go with him,' she suddenly announced, and Douglas stared at her in astonishment.

'You're as bad as he is. You're not an archaeologist or anything like it. You're a doctor.'

'Not yet,' Alisa reminded him, 'but I will be eventually. And that gives me a good idea. Every expedition needs a doctor. No problem. If everything is arranged as far as you say then nothing will stop him. Therefore I go with him and watch his step.'

'*I* want to go with him!' Douglas told her indignantly. 'Why do you think I was chasing him all morning? At this late stage there's not going to be room for more people, and if there is then I'm going. He's *my* prof. I'm doing his course.'

'You'll have to stand down. Because if there's a gap, I'm in it,' Alisa stated immovably.

'This is no way to treat your boyfriend,' Douglas snapped, and she eyed him sceptically.

'Friend is the word you're looking for,' she assured him. 'There's a subtle difference between friend and boyfriend. I like the subtleties of this life.'

'I'll look after him if I get on the trip,' Douglas promised urgently, but she shook her head and made for the door.

'Impossible. Nobody can guard him but me. He's a very difficult man.'

The door slammed and Douglas stared at it angrily. The professor wasn't the only person who was difficult. It seemed to run in the family. He shot out after her, but already he knew that he had lost. If Alisa set her mind on something it might just as well surrender right away.

Professor Fenton looked up in surprise as a blue-eyed, fair-haired whirlwind entered his study, and he sat back in his chair to observe her.

'Dear child! Whatever is wrong?' he exclaimed, and she sank down in the seat opposite his desk and looked at him sternly.

'Uncle Bill, I cannot allow you to go to Bolivia alone,' she announced.

'That's all right, then,' he assured her, his eyes crinkling with amusement. 'There'll be quite a few others with me.'

He studied her animated face, his lips twitching. She had no idea how astonishingly beautiful she was. That hair was like real gold, hanging down her back in a thick plait that almost reached her waist. He had seen her in action on the medical wing—white coat, stethoscope, her hair wound round her head—but it hadn't made one jot of difference. She had her mother's delicate beauty—the sapphire eyes, the dark arched brows, the quirky, intelligent mouth. Her mother's beauty and her father's drive. She was formidable, but she looked like a water-colour from a book of angels.

'You never told me,' she accused him, and his own dark brows shot up in surprise.

'Never told you about Bolivia?' he exclaimed. 'Dear child, I distinctly remember discussing it with you in great detail. It was over dinner, weeks ago.'

'It was probably some other poor female,' Alisa said, looking at him with reproof. 'I would never have agreed and you know that.'

'I'm certain you did, but in any case it's all arranged and it's costing a fortune. Much too late to pull out now.'

There was a rather smug sound to his voice. For a second he seemed to have a distinct twinkle in his eyes, and Alisa looked at him suspiciously but dismissed her suspicions almost instantly. He would never try to trick her. Not Uncle Bill. He was much too unworldly.

'I'll have to go with you,' she pointed out adamantly, but he shook his head slowly, pursing his lips as he dismissed that option.

'Too difficult for a woman. Not possible.'

'I'm tough as boots,' Alisa said vehemently. 'And in any case I'm almost a doctor. This expedition could need me.'

'We have a doctor,' her uncle stated with a good deal of satisfaction, as if he had thought it out well in advance.

'I'll be forced to cancel this thing, Uncle Bill,' she said dramatically, taking another tack. 'It's quite unsafe for you. I'm worried enough to take unusual action. You must drop out or I might even inform the university that you're no longer safe to be on these expeditions. I care about you a great deal.'

This time he couldn't keep the laughter out of his eyes, and he couldn't stop the wide grin that came to his face.

'It's privately financed—nothing to do with the university, other than that they'll get the backwash of any glory, should any arise. Your hands are tied this time, Alisa. You'll just have to trust to my instinct to survive.'

Alisa looked at him frustratedly, biting at her lip, and he looked back blandly, waiting for her next move.

'I'll ask the expedition leader to let me come,' she announced.

'He hates women,' her uncle said cheerfully. 'He made one rule only—no women in any capacity.'

Momentarily defeated, Alisa stood, came round to kiss his cheek, and then left with a frown on her face. The professor leaned back and let the laughter come out. His adored niece was becoming more like a prison warder every day. It was time she settled to romance.

He pursed his lips and gave it some thought. Who was that pleasant young chap who had been trying to catch his eye in this morning's lecture? Ellis! That was it. He had seen Alisa with that young man often. There was always room for a good student on these trips. He would contact the boy, because he knew that one way or another Alisa would be in Bolivia when the time came and he would be much too busy to look after her. Ellis could do that, and it might just jolly things along on the romance side.

Two weeks later Alisa sat with Uncle Bill and Douglas as they flew out to La Paz. It had taken a lot of exhausting persuasion to fix things but she was here, and she could keep an eye on her uncle right from the start. Douglas was pleased because the professor had actually sought him out and asked if he would like to be on the expedition, and as soon as his own position had been secure he had helped Alisa to work out her plans.

Uncle Bill had been suspiciously easy to manage, but as he had stressed that the leader would not countenance having a woman along Alisa was inclined to believe him. She had solved that with no difficulty. She would disguise herself as a young man. And as they approached La Paz she went along to change—a charade she had rehearsed several times with Douglas.

He had suggested that she cut her hair, but the thought was an outrage to Alisa and she had settled for a cap to cover the thick, golden tresses she had grown from childhood. It was not unusual, she told herself as she fixed her hair in the mirror at the toilet. Lots of people wore a cap nowadays—even women; it seemed to be the fashion.

Later, as she made her way back down the plane to her uncle and Douglas, she ignored the surprise in the eyes of her fellow passengers.

She had walked along there in a dress, her hair loose around her shoulders, and now she was in khaki trousers and shirt, with a very masculine watch around her wrist and her hair pinned up under a red baseball cap. Every trace of make-up was gone, and she could only hope that she looked like a rather slim young man. Douglas nodded his approval but her uncle looked doubtful.

Alisa knew that it wouldn't bother either of them if this woman-hating leader turned her around and packed her off as soon as he saw her. But she would not go without a fight and both her companions knew that, so, to a certain extent, she could rely on them.

'How do I look?' She sank down beside them and waited for the verdict.

'Like a very feminine young man,' Douglas pointed out. 'Trouble is, no boy in the world has a face like that.'

'Oh, I don't know. Some tribal youths are quite beautiful,' the professor murmured, glancing at her. 'Still, I'm inclined to agree with Douglas; you'll not get past the initial introduction.'

'Then I'll be taken sick until we're on our way,' Alisa insisted, and her uncle looked more sceptical than ever.

'Not exactly an asset to a team going into rough country,' he averred. 'We'll have to see what happens. Maybe he won't take a lot of notice.'

It was Douglas's turn to look sceptical as he glanced at Alisa's finely boned, delicate face. The blue eyes were edged with thick, dark lashes, her complexion was near perfect and, though she was fairly tall, the willowy figure was softly feminine. It was hidden now by the mannish clothes, but the face could not be disguised. This chap would have to be a woman-hater of prodigious proportions to dismiss Alisa at a glance.

He felt sorry for her because he knew that she would be on the next plane out of here, but the closer he had been to the prof, the more he thought that Alisa was wrong about his capabilities. Professor Fenton looked very competent indeed as far as he could see. It was just Alisa's mother-hen complex. He grinned at her and got a suspicious frown.

'Do you think this man will expect me to have more formal clothes for the hotel?' she asked, suddenly realising that while she had planned her expedition outfits she had given no thought to either before or after.

'Lucas? No,' her uncle assured her immediately. 'This hotel is well out of La Paz, quite off the beaten track. It's just a good clean place, an easy starting point for anyone wanting to go into the Andes. It's already high enough as it is. We'll only be there one night and then we'll be off. Lucas will be similarly attired himself. He won't give it a thought.'

Alisa hoped not. Her uncle had waxed eloquent about this man Lucas, but it had all been professional talk, expedition talk, and she had no idea what sort of man he was or why he had been chosen to lead instead of her uncle. All she knew was his unreasonable attitude to women, and that was enough to put anyone off.

As to clothes, she had brought a couple of dresses just in case she failed and had to fly back home, but they were well down in her suitcase and she was hoping to leave them at the hotel. When they got back to civilisation she would change into a dress and smile triumphantly at the daunting Mr Lucas. It would be a blow to his ego and a victory for the female of the species.

For now, her khaki trousers were loose enough to cover her figure and her firm, high breasts were well concealed beneath the equally loose khaki shirt. All she had to do was keep her head down until they were too far from any town for her to be turned back ignominiously.

* * *

The foyer of the hotel was neither large nor impressive, and Alisa, still buoyed up after the drive from the airport in La Paz, breathed a sigh of relief that there was no apparent welcoming committee. There was no appearance of formality either, and that was one worry out of the way. It looked a bit like some place from the old Wild West, and they would not be objects of any sort of curiosity.

'Ah! It is Professor Fenton and his party!' The hotel manager came across as they entered and Alisa guessed that he had recognised them from the amount of bags they had—rucksacks, backpacks and all manner of equipment that could only belong to a party of people heading out into the mountains.

'The others are here already, Professor, and I have been told to let you know that there will be a meeting at seven. We are keeping the small *sala* clear for you.' He shook her uncle's hand vigorously. 'It is a great pleasure to have you back with us.'

'You've been here before?' Alisa queried as they sped up to their rooms in an old, grinding lift.

'Several times,' her uncle told her airily. 'How do you think I manage to study any land without visiting it?'

'But recently?' Alisa persisted. 'He still remembers you.'

'Well, of course he does, my dear. I was here about four months ago.' Alisa was stunned. That made it about December, just after Christmas, when he had disappeared for three weeks and returned with a gleam in his eyes. She hadn't realised he could be so devious. That trip was supposed to have been to Holland, for a conference.

She glanced at him reproachfully and then tightened her lips, saying nothing, but the atmosphere didn't seem to bother her uncle. He ignored it. She consoled herself with the probability that he had not been far from the hotel on his earlier trip here. It had most likely been to meet this Lucas person and look the place over—maybe they had flown out from England together?

Alisa was still turning things over in her mind later as she got ready to go down to the room where she would have to face a close inspection. Once out of the confines of the university her uncle seemed to be different, not quite so easy to handle, and she had the feeling that she would have to be very circumspect in dealing with him. He had been important for a very long time, and she would never think of making him look foolish by trying to order him about in front of other people. It would just be a case of watching him closely and setting her own mind at rest.

She frowned at herself in the mirror as she fastened her hair back up on top of her head. Was she being selfish? Was that why she was here? Was all this so that she would not have it on her conscience if anything happened to Uncle Bill? He had managed his life very well without her intervention in the past, and she remembered welcoming him back after trips like this many times. He had always arrived home looking healthy and pleased with himself. Now she was proposing to treat him like a doddery old man.

Alisa pulled her red cap down over her hair and tucked the last strands away. The frown was still there; so were the doubts. Uncle Bill was indulging her, she was becoming more sure of that by the minute. But she was here and her worries had not lessened, and neither had her conviction that he needed her. Whether she could pass herself off as a young man in front of Mr Lucas was another matter.

She turned and looked at herself sideways in the mirror and loosened the shirt at the waist. It would have been a decided advantage to be flat-chested at this moment, and she even considered tying something round her breasts to conceal them. It would be too uncomfortable, though—especially if they were going to walk for days. She had no idea what transport would be provided. Her uncle had been very vague when questioned, and she again had the uneasy thought that he was either making fun of her or setting out to teach her a lesson.

Luckily she did not have to go down alone. Both Douglas and her uncle came to collect her as the appointed time arrived, and they went down to the small *sala* together. She didn't feel quite so conspicuous like that, and was greatly relieved when her uncle introduced her to the other man who was already there.

'This is Jeff Lane. He's been with us before and he takes pictures, among other things.'

Alisa found herself facing a tough-looking man who had very humorous eyes, and she knew that this was the first hurdle.

'One of my students, Douglas Ellis,' her uncle said, getting on with the introductions, 'and this is my young nephew, Alex. He—er—he's a medical student—very useful to us.'

Jeff Lane seemed to accept things at face value and Alisa breathed more easily, trying to avoid Douglas's eyes. He seemed to be more nervous about this than she was. They had rehearsed things but this was the first time that the deception had been put to the test, and it had been more smoothly executed than she had believed possible. Uncle Bill was a man with more talents than she'd imagined, and Alisa found herself regarding him a little warily.

Jeff Lane was tanned and fit-looking, obviously a photographer by the look of his equipment, and he had the lithe way of moving that she automatically knew belonged to a man who was used to mountains. He didn't even look at her closely, he was too impressed by her uncle, and she felt safe at last.

It was her uncle who shattered that illusion.

'Ah! Here's Lucas!' he exclaimed with great satisfaction, turning to the door with a wide smile as a man came into the room from the foyer. 'Now we can start.'

Alisa looked up, and then felt as if the ground was slipping away from under her. She had not really given much thought to the man she had taken such pains to deceive. Other than a purely instinctive dislike she had never bothered to imagine how he would look, and he took her completely by surprise. Her heart began to pound alarmingly, because she was not so sure now that she would get past the inspection of those eyes.

For now, he had not actually looked at her—she was just one of a group of people and he was taken up at the moment with her uncle—but she knew the time would come, and she felt a burst of resentment to add to her anxiety. Why should he have the power to turn her away? Her uncle was the important one here. This trip would never have been organised or financed if her uncle had not had such a world-wide reputation.

She turned to Douglas for support but, like the others, he was on his feet ready to meet the newcomer, and as her uncle turned back to the room Alisa made herself face the man who towered over her uncle, dwarfing him with his lean, muscular height. The face was darker than she had expected, and hard, suntanned even darker than the man she had recently met. His hair was utterly black, thick and silky-looking, and his dark eyes flickered over them all, making a lightning assessment.

As he noticed Alisa the hard mouth hardened even more, and she was greatly relieved when her uncle went into action.

'Just two newcomers,' he said. 'Last-minute additions to the party. This is Douglas Ellis, a very good student of mine.' There was a moment of respite as the man murmured politely to Douglas, and then it could be put off no longer. 'This is my nephew Alex,' Uncle Bill introduced smoothly, not even blinking at the outright untruth. 'He's a medical student—likely to be useful.'

'Possibly.' The cool face turned to Alisa, the eyes regarding her dispassionately. They were brown, she noticed, not black as she had at first thought, and she wasn't having a lot of success in looking away. She dared not drop her head, it would be too feminine an act, and to her consternation he seemed to be inspecting her minutely. 'You have the name of your uncle?' he queried. 'You are also called Fenton?'

Alisa gulped and tried to make her voice deep.

'Yes,' she managed huskily, and the dark brows rose ironically at her tone.

'This is Lucas Sanchez, Alex,' her uncle interposed swiftly as he saw her nerve slipping, and it dawned on her then. She suddenly knew the reason for the dark face, the silky black hair and the small, barely discernible accent. He was not, as she had earlier supposed, English. He was Bolivian. Lucas was his first name, not his surname, and she looked up at him with startled eyes.

'My mother is English,' he remarked, as if he had an uncanny ability to read her mind. 'My father is Bolivian. Welcome to my country, Dr Fenton.' He gave her a very ironical look and Alisa pulled herself together, quite shaken that he had assessed the way she was looking at him.

'I'm not exactly a doctor yet,' she muttered, managing to move her eyes from his rather satanic face.

'No doubt you will get there,' he murmured, turning away and dismissing her. She was very glad that he had. Much more of his intent scrutiny and she would have been confessing everything. Her uncle must be close to this man, because she had never heard him address anyone before other than by their surname. That was how she had made the mistake. She realised that she was mulling this over with an almost delirious relief that he was now concerning himself with others.

Eventually they were all seated, the atmosphere relaxed and casual. Lucas Sanchez lay back in an armchair, one booted foot crossed over his knee as he glanced at all of them.

'Make yourselves comfortable and Professor Fenton will tell you as much as we know at this moment,' he invited. 'We have kept this expedition small because it affords more secrecy, and as you are all capable of doing more than one job other people were not necessary. The porters will meet us when we are closer to the mountains and from there we will be secure from prying eyes. It will often be tough going, and I hope that the new arrivals from England realise that. We are short of only one thing—time. Therefore it will not be possible to coax anyone along. You start and you finish. Otherwise you return alone.'

He glanced sideways at Alisa, the dark eyes drifting over her without even a question in them, but she knew that he was doubtful about her ability to keep pace with the others. Even Douglas was tough, and while she could disguise herself she could not disguise her lighter frame.

'I'll keep up,' she heard herself say, and Lucas Sanchez gave her another glance, his lips twisting sardonically.

'I do not doubt it,' he stated. 'Your uncle would not have brought you otherwise. Young men are pretty resilient. I remember being a youth myself, and students nowadays take on some unusual and exhausting activities, I believe. In any case,' he added drily, 'if you should need to return to the hotel and the airport at La Paz, I am sure you will manage it alone.'

It sounded more like a threat than encouragement, and Alisa was delighted when her uncle began to speak. He never had any difficulty in talking, especially about his own beloved subject, and seconds later they were all spellbound—even the sardonic Sanchez. After one more sceptical glance at her he sat with narrowed eyes and simply listened.

He had strong-looking hands, she noted, almost artistic, nevertheless, with long fingers and well-shaped nails. The high cheekbones were now explained. He was South American, probably some descendant of the Spaniards or the indigenous people who had lived here long ago.

The thick black hair was indicative of that. The eyes were not quite black enough, though. They would have been almost beautiful if he hadn't been so hard-looking. Probably his mother had brown eyes, or, if not, her English blood had watered down the matt black of the other eyes she had seen since she had been here.

He was impressive but not at all pleasant, and even though her uncle was doing the talking this man was quite clearly the most important person here, and she wondered what qualifications allowed him to be the leader and to take the attitude he had taken since his arrival in the room.

'As most of you know,' her uncle began, 'La Paz is at the edge of the *altiplano* or high plateau formed by the Andes. The land here is nothing like the semi-tropical valleys below. You will get used to the thin air, but even those who come here often have to take it easy to begin with—so no undue rushing about. At first we go slowly, and the newcomers can enjoy the sight of the snow-capped Andes because we will be going upwards all the time.

'A mighty civilisation was once spread over this plain, with great buildings and monuments. It was started by the Aymaras and continued by the Incas, who came here somewhere around the eleventh century. The coming of the Spaniards altered all that, and when they discovered silver here the old social system was destroyed by Spanish colonisation. The native peoples were pushed out onto higher, unfertile land.

'That is where we are going, because I believe there are still ruins to find and Señor Sanchez agrees with me. It is possible that extremely precious or religious possessions were taken higher into the mountains, where they could be safely hidden. We have both explored this region before, but never in any depth and never with great success. However, we still believe that there is much to find, and lately rumours have been circulating about the past that have interested others. We hope to get there first and to get there secretly. It is for this reason that Señor Sanchez is financing this expedition.'

Alisa hardly heard anything else. Lucas Sanchez was leading this expedition because he was financing it. Money gave him the right to dictate. She glanced at him surreptitiously and frowned bleakly. Yes, he looked wealthy. He looked easily sure of himself. She had to admit that it was not just money that gave him that air. He looked physically capable of any amount of hardship, and as he stood at that moment, gracefully uncoiling himself from the deep chair, Alisa felt a qualm of unease at the sight of his tall, athletic frame.

If he spotted her for a female she was in trouble, because no amount of either pleading or badgering would change his mind. He would just say, No women! and get rid of her. He looked chauvinistic, and as the dark eyes turned in her direction Alisa spun round and started an animated conversation with Douglas, who was unlucky enough to be close at the time.

'Calm down,' he muttered, gripping her arm. 'You've made it. He never noticed your sex at all. He's only concerned with the trip. Everything is going to be just fine.'

Alisa's heartbeats subsided. She supposed that he was right. After all, Lucas Sanchez had looked her right in the face and accepted her uncle's word. So why did she doubt it? Why was she so much on edge? It was probably the certain knowledge that if she failed on the trek, he would send her back here alone and not give one momentary thought to any danger she might encounter on the way. After all, he had threatened it, and he did not look like a man who made idle threats.

CHAPTER TWO

HE WAS speaking now and Alisa quickly tuned herself in to his words, scared to miss even one syllable.

'Apart from those of us gathered here there is one more member who will arrive tomorrow very early,' he stated. 'He is José García—Dr García.' He glanced at Alisa as he said that, and she managed a weak smile which he ignored. 'I suggest that we retire now, get an early night and be fresh for our start in the morning.'

They were dismissed, and Alisa couldn't get out of the room fast enough. So far so good, but it didn't quite feel like that. It didn't even feel like all right for now. The only safe place was a long way from the daunting leader, and she didn't need basic feminine instincts to tell her that. There was something about his voice that was like the black warning of distant thunder.

Her uncle joined her as she frantically sought the lift, afraid that Lucas Sanchez might be going up at the same time, and he was very elated. He also looked very sure of himself, horribly capable, and Alisa asked herself what on earth she was doing here when she could have been joining a cycling trip to the Black Forest with a few of her friends. This was not really her idea of the best way to spend the last vacation before hospital training.

And as to retiring and getting an early night, she was wound up like a top. One glance of inspection assured her that her uncle Bill was blissfully happy and completely in control of himself. She felt like pointing out that if she was discovered he would have some tricky questions to answer, but she managed to keep silent. It was no use trying to make anyone else feel insecure. One case of shattered nerves was enough for any expedition.

It seemed to Alisa's irritated and anxious mind that both her uncle and Douglas went off to bed like two happy and excited schoolboys who had been ordered to go to sleep by a stern but admired headmaster. Once at their floor, they went trotting off in opposite directions, with merry promises to meet on the morrow, and Alisa looked after them with stormy eyes.

Most likely on the morrow that same scrupulously fair headmaster would order her on the next flight out of here. She went into her room and looked at herself in the mirror. Had she really fooled him? He didn't look at all easy to fool. The trousers and shirt hid her figure, and the cap hid her hair, but nothing had been hiding her face—and it was not a man's face, not even a boy's face.

She tugged at the cap and decided that it looked as if it was concealing something. There was too much hair crammed underneath it, and, even plaited and wound round her head, the sheer volume of it filled the red cap unnaturally. When she took the cap off her disguise faded away completely. She just looked like an untidy female walker.

Maybe with another man she would have got away with this, but she could not settle to the idea that Lucas Sanchez was in any way gullible. She sighed with irritation. What was wrong with her? She *had* got away with it. He had looked at her, spoken to her, and even called her a youth or something like it. There was no need whatever to be so nervy and apprehensive.

All the same, she could not sleep, and she unlocked the door to her veranda, meaning to stand outside for a few minutes. The moon was bright, a silver globe in the dark sky, and there was not a cloud in sight. Even in the bright moonlight the stars were visible—large, glittering and incredibly close. It was an illusion, she knew, something to do with the still, thin air and the proximity of the mountains.

They rose in towering peaks, snow-topped and majestic, and Alisa stood for a few minutes gazing at them in awe. The Andes! She had heard so much about them since she was a child, about the people who lived beneath their lofty heights. She had dreamed of this massive chain of rock that stretched so far on this side of South America, of the wildlife and the high Lake Titicaca, almost two miles in the air and the highest inland sea in the world. She had listened to tales of Chile and Peru and the soaring flight of the great condor, the spirit of the Andes.

Alisa shivered in the cold night air, hugging her arms around her body, and suddenly the nerves went, her anxiety left her. She *wanted* to be here! She wanted to see the places her uncle had told her about when she was young enough to sit on his knee and listen wide-eyed to his tales. It was like destiny. She was as happy as her uncle, as anxious to be off as he was, and any uneasy feelings of being selfish drifted away.

Steps led from her balcony to the garden of the hotel, and after a quick look down she decided that it was probably a very civilised place, even though it was small and well out of La Paz. The gardens were floodlit and plenty of tourists came here all the year round. There was not much chance of any mishap if she had a short, brisk walk before bed. She closed the door to her room, pocketed the key and went silently down the steps to the rough lawn below.

The garden was informal, with trees and bushes—the floodlighting catching the shine of the leaves and the moon silvering the rough bark. It was peaceful, with a faint trace of some scented flower that she did not recognise, and Alisa drew in a deep, contented breath. Tomorrow the adventure would begin, and after one brisk stroll round this part of the garden she would go back to the balcony and let herself into her room.

This time she knew that she would sleep, because the flight and the trauma of her meeting with the unnerving leader of the expedition were rapidly catching up with her. Nobody had ever worried her so much before—in fact not many people worried her at all. There was something about this man, though, that made her feel nothing but anxiety. Thank goodness he was safely in his bed. As he had advised everyone else to get an early night he would certainly be doing that himself, even though he looked tough enough to climb for a week without food or sleep.

'It is unwise to wander about alone in a strange place,' a deep voice admonished. A dark figure detached itself from the shadows and Alisa's heart skipped a beat as she recognised the tall, athletic frame of Lucas Sanchez. 'Young men are inclined to reckless behaviour, as I remember,' he continued. 'However, as you are a member of my expedition, I urge you to take more care and I strongly recommend that you return to your room and lock the door.'

'I—I was having a last-minute walk,' Alisa stammered, wanting to take to her heels and put a lot of distance between them. She was heartily glad that she had put the cap back on, because even in this light his dark eyes seemed to be piercing.

'I alarmed you, even though you know me?' he enquired in taunting surprise as he heard her uneasy voice. 'That does not exactly fit in with your bold decision to leave your room and pace about alone in the grounds of the hotel at night.'

He was much closer now, and Alisa was utterly incapable of moving. Any action would make him even more suspicious. He stopped and stared down at her, his face even more satanic-looking in the mixture of peculiar light from the moon and the floodlighting that edged the trees.

'Or perhaps you are only afraid of me?' he questioned in a softly menacing voice.

'Of course not!' Alisa managed sharply. 'In any case, I'm quite capable of taking care of myself.'

'*Are* you?' His hand shot out and captured her, his hard fingers curling round her wrist. 'You are telling me, Alex Fenton, that you could take on two or three robbers intent on stealing that very powerful-looking watch?'

Alisa glanced down at the watch. It was supposed to be her outward sign of masculinity, and she wondered uneasily if she had overdone it a bit there. It was like a small clock—too big and heavy for her slender wrist.

'According to my uncle,' she said briskly, remembering to deepen her voice, 'the people in Bolivia are friendly and helpful.'

'Thank you,' he murmured in the same dark, taunting manner. 'It is good of you to mention it. However, we are not all alike. Some of us are more dangerous than others.'

Alisa knew that very well. He was definitely one of the dangerous ones, and she couldn't take this any longer. She muttered goodnight, turning rapidly, with every intention of racing to her room and locking the door.

She never even made two steps, because his hands came down on her shoulders as she turned and, before she could struggle, his long, strong fingers were probing the delicate bones he discovered there, sliding slowly across her collarbone and upwards over the silken skin of her neck. Shock raced through her like electric sparks.

For a moment her breath seemed to stop, as if she had never been touched before in her life.

'How dare you?' Alisa gasped. She swallowed convulsively, trying to get rid of the peculiar clenching in her stomach, and he spun her round to face him, his expression forbidding, his eyes glittering like black crystal.

'What a very feminine statement of outrage,' he said icily. 'But then, you are very feminine indeed, are you not, Señorita Fenton?'

Before she could stop him, her cap was snatched off and tossed to the ground. He was still holding her by the shoulder, and his next undertaking was easily accomplished. He flicked the long pins from her hair and the heavy golden braid fell forward across her shoulder, sliding silkily over his hand and coming to rest almost at her waist.

He looked down at it steadily for a second while Alisa wondered where her breath had gone and what had happened to her to make her feel so utterly shaken. She looked very pale in the moonlight, and the light from the hotel caught the blue of her eyes, making them shine like the bewildered gaze of a scared and trapped animal. His dark eyes rose slowly to meet hers and she blurted out just anything to get her self-control back.

'I can explain!' She got no further. The dark eyes narrowed ominously.

'Tomorrow you will be on the first flight out of here,' he commanded coldly.

'But my uncle—'

'Is an old friend of mine, but obviously over-indulgent with you. He is also absent-minded when the mood takes him. It is not too long ago that he proudly showed me a photograph of his niece, Alisa. I have a very good memory, *señorita*, and he never mentioned that his niece had a twin. I have not the slightest doubt that you bullied him into this madness. Nevertheless, it has been a waste of time. You leave in the morning.'

'You don't understand.' Alisa looked up at him with pleading eyes. 'Uncle Bill can't take care of himself.'

If anything, that remark made him more coldly angry than before, and his hand tightened cruelly on her shoulder.

'Now it is my turn to say "How dare you?", *señorita*,' he bit out. He pointed to the white-capped Andes. 'If he so desired, Professor Fenton could climb those peaks. I have known him for many years and he is not in any way lessened by his age. You, on the other hand, do not even have sufficient common sense to stay in your room when the night is cold and the moon shows your exact whereabouts. No doubt you are always filled with this outrageous confidence. Your uncle will be digging up the past and climbing the rocks when you are lying beneath some bush, beaten and robbed. You will be on tomorrow's flight! Now go to your room!'

He raised his voice to ice-splintering volume, and Alisa didn't try any more entreaties. His chauvinistic insolence brought her speedily down to earth and her blue eyes flashed like sapphires in the light.

'If I'm not on the expedition then you have nothing to do with me at all!' she blazed. 'But I'm going! Not because you're ordering me to go but because in my room I'll not be able to hear your overbearing arrogance. If my uncle is your friend, then it just shows his lack of judgement, and if anything happens to him on this trip I'll be back here and after you before you can say Jack Robinson!'

'I have never felt the inclination to say Jack Robinson.' He stared down at her disdainfully. 'Stay here or go to your room as you choose. In the morning you will leave

Bolivia. If, in the meantime, you have been robbed and beaten, I will arrange to have a nurse accompany you. But whether you are fit or sadly injured, you will be on that flight, Señorita Fenton!'

He turned away and walked off with a cold imperiousness that enraged Alisa almost enough for her to throw herself at him and tear at his shirt with sharp, angry fingers. Caution stayed her, though. He might just be the one to beat her and leave her under a bush. She glared after him and then looked round a little fearfully as he passed out of sight.

It was very quiet here. His presence was so commanding that now he had gone the silence seemed to scream at her. She scooped up her cap, ran to the steps and raced up to her room, unlocking the door and hurrying inside. She was careful to lock it afterwards, and it was only as she was trying the handle for the fourth time that she realised how he had unnerved her.

He was a monster—a cold-blooded, arrogant monster. All the same, she knew when she was defeated, and it was no use appealing to her uncle. If he had shown that photograph to the lordly Señor Sanchez then he had known all along that she would be unmasked. He was either forgetful or deceitful. Señor Sanchez couldn't have it both ways, and she remembered only too well how her uncle had laughed when she had threatened him in his study at the university.

She remembered, too, how easily he had given in later. It had been done to humiliate her; probably Douglas was in on it too. He would have given anything to be here, and if she hadn't intervened her uncle would never have invited Douglas on this trip.

Alisa went to sleep with very malevolent thoughts running round in her head. Every one of them was directed at a man but mostly they were directed at Lucas

Sanchez, and it was galling to know that she could not do one thing to get the better of him. His power was absolute, apparently, and she already knew that absolute power corrupted absolutely. If that hadn't been the case he would never have touched her in that disgraceful way.

Tomorrow she would have to be on that flight whether she liked it or not, and Uncle Bill would shake his head sadly and then go about his business, putting her completely out of his mind.

Next morning, when her uncle and Douglas called for her to escort her down to breakfast, they found Alisa all ready. She was dressed in a softly pleated dress that had tiny flowers strewn over a cream background. Her hair was loose and shining like a golden cape as it hung down her back. With strappy sandals on her feet and her face delicately made up she looked excessively feminine, and, angry though she was, she felt a wave of satisfaction when her uncle just stared at her, his mouth almost hanging open.

'Alisa!' he exclaimed. 'What are you doing? The whole pack of us leave as soon as Dr García arrives, and, in any case, appear like that and Lucas will send you packing.'

'He already has done,' Alisa informed him crossly. 'I encountered him last night while you were both curled up in your beds.'

'How? Where?' her uncle asked. 'What were you doing wandering about? Apart from the risk, it was just asking for trouble to let him have a better look at you.'

'Oh, the trouble was already waiting for me,' Alisa assured him, staring at him angrily. 'He was never fooled for one minute. He was just storing up sufficient humiliation before he pounced. And I'm not one bit surprised as he had already seen a photograph of me—the one you showed him when you were here last.'

'Did I?' Uncle Bill mused, shaking his head thoughtfully. 'It really must have slipped my mind.'

'Oh, do stop it!' Alisa snapped. 'I'm beginning to realise that nothing slips your mind. But I'm very annoyed with you. This has made me look like a fool, and your precious Señor Sanchez pointed out in no uncertain terms that you are about ten times more capable than I am. According to him, you'll still be making these trips when I'm lying battered and bruised under some foreign hedge!'

The professor had the grace to look sheepish, but Douglas was innocent. Alisa could tell that by the way he stood there looking utterly stunned. Everything was down to her uncle, and she turned annoyed and reproachful eyes on him, waiting for his explanation.

'I have to plead guilty,' he confessed, and she tightened her lips and glared at him.

'Why did you do it?' she demanded. 'Do you enjoy seeing me humiliated?'

'Alisa, my dear child, of course I don't,' he protested. 'But you are such a strong-willed person, and determined to have your own way. I know you mean well, but you really don't know everything. This trip is not exactly dangerous but it will be physically exhausting, and I really feel worried about you.'

'I told you, I'm tough as a boot!' she snapped, and he smiled his usual little smile of affection.

'You don't look like a boot, my dear. You sometimes look quite fragile. Betsy and I have often worried about you.'

Alisa looked dumbfounded and Douglas seemed to be nodding his head in sombre agreement.

'Shut up!' she warned him, before he could open his mouth. 'This is a family dispute.' She turned back to her uncle but his affectionate face got the better of her, and she knew perfectly well that she did bulldoze her way into things if she had her mind made up.

'Never mind,' she sighed, giving him a hug. 'At least I've seen the Andes. Your esteemed leader has ordered me out on the first flight and I seem to be stuck with that. But,' she added with a look of stern rebuke, 'I think you could have said all this in England.'

'Given half the chance, I would have done,' her uncle said mildly.

'I can't undertake to look after you again,' she warned. 'This has been a lesson I'll not forget.' She looked at him seriously. 'You'll have to take care, because I don't expect you'll get any sympathy from that Sanchez man if you hurt yourself. Now, let's get down to breakfast and I just hope he's not there.'

'You're misjudging him, Alisa,' the professor cautioned as they left. 'Lucas Sanchez is a very unusual man. He's giving money and time to this, as he does to lots of things for his country. He doesn't need the glory either. He's rich beyond most people's dreams.'

'Slaves and gun-running, I bet!' Alisa snorted, making for the lift.

'Mining, cattle and coffee,' the professor corrected. 'He's important.'

'I know,' Alisa snapped. 'He practically told me!'

Just the thought of him had her fuming, especially as she remembered the particular way he had chosen to unmask her. This morning the odd feeling had gone and she was simply furious. It hadn't been at all necessary. He could have just announced that he knew who she was. There had been no need for him to touch her, no need for him to run his hands over her shoulders and neck like that. She certainly didn't want to see him again, because apart from anything else it would be embarrassing.

Unfortunately he was there, just finishing his breakfast as they went into the dining room, and his dark eyes captured her the moment she stepped through the door. She just had time to notice how his glance flashed over her from head to foot before she looked haughtily away. She felt her face flushing, and as soon as she could she turned her back on him. He was the sort of man to get under your guard in one way or another, but luckily she would be out of here soon. He could order everyone else about.

He came across to their table as soon as he had finished his own meal and obviously wanted a word with her uncle.

'I am still waiting to hear from Dr García. He should have been here already, but as yet there is no sign of him. If he does not arrive soon we will be late in leaving.'

He ignored Alisa and she bridled at the rudeness. He was ruthlessly cutting her out, as if she wasn't there at all. Of course, if he *had* spoken to her it would have been awkward, she conceded, because he was not a man to bend at all and she was still infuriated by his actions of the previous night.

'Can we leave without García?' her uncle enquired, and Lucas Sanchez shook his dark head emphatically.

'No. I would not risk it. I am not expecting any problems, but there will be the four of us and there will also be the porters. To risk going into the mountains with no medical assistance would be unwise. We must wait for García, however late he is.'

'We're pressed for time,' her uncle reminded him, and Sanchez admitted that.

'I agree, but the risk is too great to take. What do we do if someone is injured? It may be some small thing that a doctor could deal with easily. We have our medical supplies, but none of us are competent to use them adequately. We really must wait for García.'

The professor reluctantly agreed, and Alisa was greatly relieved when the tall, powerful persecutor with night-black hair turned to leave. He glanced down at her, catching her look of blue-eyed fury, but his dark face showed no sign of recognition. He remembered his manners, though. He bowed his head slightly in acknowledgement of her presence. Even that action was performed with a natural arrogance that made her blood boil.

There was still no word of the doctor as they finished breakfast, and her uncle seemed to spend a lot of time looking at his watch. Douglas was very subdued because he seemed to feel guilty about Alisa, and she had to make an effort to be especially nice to him. It was not his fault that she had met such an inflexible, cold-blooded man.

She wound her arm in his as they crossed the foyer on the way to the lift.

'I'll survive,' she promised. 'The blow to my ego is not life-threatening, and there can't be more men like Sanchez about.'

'You wanted to go with us, though, Al,' Douglas commiserated, and she nodded ruefully.

'Actually, I really did in the end,' she confessed. 'And it wasn't just to look after Uncle Bill. I suddenly realised last night that I'd been dreaming about the Andes all my life. It gave me a very contented feeling to think I was about to set foot on them—even if only on the edge.'

'Oh, Al!' Douglas muttered, putting his arm round her shoulders and giving her a mournful squeeze. 'Shall I back out and go home with you?'

'Don't you dare!' Alisa warned quickly. 'You wanted to come here and I'm relying on you to watch the prof. Whatever the mighty leader says, I know my uncle better than anyone else does. He lives in the clouds, and he's quite capable of stepping off a cliff while consulting his notes.'

'I'll guard him with my life,' Douglas promised, and Alisa kissed his cheek.

'Good and noble friend,' she praised, smiling at him affectionately.

The smile died on her face when she saw that they were being observed by Lucas Sanchez. He was staring at them coldly, and as she stared back, trying to get the exact matching expression on her face, his eyes moved slowly over her, running from her shining hair to her figure in insolent appraisal, and Alisa's face began to glow with embarrassment as her expression changed from cold disinterest to furious resentment.

He noticed and his lips twisted in sardonic mockery, making it quite clear that his speculating glance had been merely to bring her to heel in a very unpleasant, masculine way. She walked into the lift and stared into space until the door closed behind her. Douglas had gone off to consult with her uncle and she had the lift to herself, luckily. It gave her the necessary privacy to allow her face to flood with colour and her hands to clench in rage.

She already knew that her flight did not leave for over two hours, and Alisa began to pack her things in a desultory manner, pausing frequently to stand on the balcony and gaze at the snow-capped mountains. She was bitterly disappointed. She knew that she would never again come so close to something she had dreamed of for most of her life. So close and yet not close enough. In her mind she could picture the others climbing in the sun, could imagine the cold nights and the constant sight of towering peaks.

They might even see the mighty condor soaring overhead in its easy, effortless flight. She didn't know how far they were going. Before coming here her only thoughts had been of how to outwit the man who had ordered that there be no women in the party. Well, she had not outwitted him, and the idea of going home came as a sad let-down after her hopes of the previous night.

There was her uncle too. She had loved him all her life. She had had nobody else to love. His house had been her refuge since she was a baby and left without parents. Her bachelor uncle had manfully coped with her upbringing. Whatever Señor Sanchez thought, she felt a very strong need to protect him—but now she had to rely on Douglas, who was not altogether practical himself.

Alisa jumped and came out of her state of miserable musing as a sharp tap on the door warned her that she was about to have company. It would be Uncle Bill, she knew, and she quickly composed her face. There was no need for him to know how disappointed she was. It was better for him to go on thinking that she was as tough as she claimed to be.

She opened the door, smiling, but her smile faded rapidly as she found herself facing Lucas Sanchez, and her lips tightened angrily when she assumed he had come to remind her to catch the plane.

'What do you want?' she snapped, glaring up at him. It was a long way up too, and she resented that he was so strongly masculine and superior. 'You have nothing to do with me whatever now, and if I choose to miss the plane and catch one next week that is my business!'

'I wish to speak to you,' he stated calmly, not at all ruffled by her manner. 'I agree that you are completely free to do as you will, but that is not why I am here.'

It dawned on Alisa that he was a little more flexible in his expression than usual, and immediately she became anxious.

'It's something wrong with Uncle Bill!' she surmised desperately. 'What's happened to him?'

'In the hotel?' he asked, looking at her askance. 'Nothing, *señorita*. How could it? You have an unreasonable fixation about your uncle's health.'

'I do not!' Alisa snapped. 'But even if I had, it's not at all unreasonable. He's the only one I have, and I care about him more than anything. Anyway,' she continued sharply, 'if it's not that, what is it? I can't imagine you've come to wish me a pleasant flight.'

'If you would allow me to come in, I will be able to tell you why I am here,' he suggested, and she looked at him with sceptical disdain.

'Simply state your reasons and go,' she suggested coldly. 'You are not the sort of person I would enjoy having a nice chat with. As it's probably some order—issue it and depart!'

She was surprised by the wry grin that came to his face. His eyes narrowed and he tilted his head on one side and looked down at her with amused speculation.

'You are not at all like the educated women of my country,' he assured her. 'You are very aggressive and hostile. This constant desire for combat should be curbed. It is time some man took you in hand and tamed you.' He straightened up while she was still digesting this with growing fury, and his sardonic amusement faded. 'In fact,' he continued steadily, 'I have come to ask a favour.'

Alisa stared at him in open-mouthed astonishment, gathering rage by the second. She had never heard such cheek in her life.

'Unless it's a request to shoot you in the foot, forget it!' she fumed. 'Do you seriously think that after last night I would do more than watch with interest if you were floating downstream in a sinking canoe?'

By some superb self-control he kept his temper, and looked down at her with intent dark eyes.

'It has become very obvious that last night I spoke too hastily,' he admitted coolly. 'I did not know then what I know now. We are in need of your services, *señorita*, and I hope you will not refuse.'

'What services?' Alisa demanded angrily. 'You pointed out last night how utterly incapable I am. How have I improved overnight?'

'You have stopped being deceitful, for one thing,' he stated icily. 'You are no longer wearing that ridiculous disguise.'

'It was my only way of joining the trip,' she snapped. 'Not that it did a lot of good.'

'You may join the trip,' he conceded with a good measure of cold magnanimity. 'If you wish to change into travelling gear and join us downstairs you may come along with the party.'

'Why?' Alisa stared at him with wide-eyed suspicion, not at all mollified by his icy concession.

'Dr García has been taken ill,' he told her. 'We need a doctor. Without one the expedition cannot go on. You are almost a doctor. You will do very well.'

'Ah!' Alisa breathed triumphantly. 'You're stuck, Señor Sanchez, and now I've become acceptable. *Now* it doesn't matter one bit that I'm female, weak, without common sense and likely to be robbed and beaten. *Now* all your mighty principles are changed without you even blinking an eye. Well, you can search around for another doctor, because I'm following your orders and going home. If you want me to go on this expedition then pull out yourself and appoint another leader, because there's no way I would even walk down the street with you!'

Alisa stepped back into the room and closed the door in his face. She was shaking with annoyance and reaction. Never in her life had she been made to feel so insignificant. His sheer audacity left her speechless.

He disliked women and her in particular. He had called her deceitful, among other things, and now, when it suited him, he had come up to her room and calmly told her that she could go on the expedition because she would 'do very well'. In other words he would put up with her. He would let her carry the medical bag and dish out aspirin. He might even, as a concession, allow her to set a broken leg, but she would probably be asked to walk behind the others and sit at the edge of the camp-fire like a second-class citizen.

No way! Even if he had begged very sincerely she would have refused, but he had not even done that. He had simply come and *informed* her that she might just about manage so long as everybody stayed fit and well. The effrontery of the man astonished her. She would rather be on the plane and winging her way back to England crying bitterly with disappointment than even glimpsing him again.

CHAPTER THREE

ALISA began to pack her belongings vigorously now, her mouth tight with temper, and when yet another knock sounded on her door later she snatched the door open, ready to do more battle. It was her uncle and Douglas, both looking more miserable than she had been feeling earlier.

'What's wrong?' she asked quickly, and they both walked in and sat down.

'The expedition is off,' her uncle told her unhappily. 'All this time, all this planning and now we can't go. García is ill and Lucas is perfectly right; it's too risky to go without medical back-up.'

Suspicion reared its head, and Alisa looked at him closely.

'Did he send you up here to pressurise me?' she asked sharply, but her uncle looked up at her with startled eyes.

'Lucas? I told you, Alisa, he said no women. He's not likely to change his mind now that you've shown him just how feminine you are.'

A quick look at Douglas confirmed that her uncle was not up to any tricks and she sat down on the bed, her brow wrinkled in a frown, her mouth tightly closed. It rather looked as if Señor Sanchez had been trying to hold the expedition together for her uncle's sake, because if he was as rich as all that he would not be bothered for himself.

She cast a sidelong glance at her uncle's face and her lips twisted ruefully. He looked like a child who had been told he could not go to the fairground. He had been buoyed up about this trip, elated. Now he would have to go back.

'What about another doctor?' she asked hopefully, but her uncle shook his head.

'Too late. Doctors have patients and appointments. They have to ask someone else to stand in for them. All of us are pressed for time. There's university for me, and for Douglas. Lucas has business commitments, and Jeff Lane is a well-meaning amateur with a life to run and work to attend. No, it's too late.'

'We'll see.' Alisa said tightly. She got up and went to the door. 'Stay here until I get back.'

'But, my dear—' the professor began, and she waved him to silence.

'Don't ask. Just don't ask,' she begged. 'I'm about to indulge in the ultimate self-sacrifice, and don't ever say that I don't love you. What I am about to do may very well choke me.'

Alisa went out to the lift without waiting for comments, because she knew that if she gave herself time to think she would just rush back to her room. Lucas Sanchez would no doubt stare at her evilly and snap her head off, but for her uncle's sake she had to try. She had to try for poor Douglas too. He had looked as if he was about to weep.

She ran Lucas Sanchez to earth in the car park of the hotel. The receptionist had directed her there and even the men at the desk had looked downcast. News, it seemed, spread rapidly here—especially if it was to do with her uncle and the great Sanchez.

He was standing by two Land Rovers, apparently about to dismiss them, and he turned as Alisa came up, looking at her without any enthusiasm. She clenched her fists and began before she could change her mind.

'All right,' she said flatly. 'I agree. I'll go.'

'You have thought it over?' he enquired, his dark, cold eyes scanning her tight expression. 'Do not do me any favours, Señorita Fenton.'

'Don't worry. I won't,' she informed him sharply. 'The reason that I've changed my mind is because of my uncle's great disappointment. For all I know this may be the last chance he has to go on any expedition.'

'Will you drop this ridiculous and morbid fixation?' he grated. 'Professor Fenton is a fit man, and if you were any sort of doctor you would know it.'

'I'm a learning sort of a doctor!' Alisa bit out, glaring up at him. 'Do you or do you not want me to go with you?'

'For myself, I do not want you within a hundred miles of me,' he growled. 'For the expedition, though, I need you. Therefore, thank you for offering your services.'

'Only because of my uncle,' Alisa reminded him heatedly, and he nodded at her, his lips in one straight line of temper.

'Está entendido,' he rasped. 'That is understood. I will inform the professor. Perhaps you would tell Señor Ellis?'

'He's in my room,' Alisa muttered, and he looked at her with icy disdain.

'Naturally.' He was even more tight-lipped and disapproving, and Alisa looked up furiously.

'They both are,' she snapped. 'They're crying on each other's shoulders. Why else do you think I'm here humiliating myself in front of a supercilious stranger?'

'I apologise,' he conceded, with very little show of being contrite. 'Perhaps you would inform both of them, in that case. I will countermand my orders here and prepare to get us rolling.'

Orders! That was what they were going to get throughout this whole trip, Alisa surmised angrily as she turned back to the hotel. For two pins she would change her mind again. The memory of her uncle's downcast face and one glimpse of the mountains stopped such thoughts, however, and she walked on, not looking back.

'One hour at the latest!' he called after her sharply, and she turned her head to scowl at him, stilling her tongue by sheer willpower. This was going to be the worst few weeks of her life. In future she would keep well out of her uncle's affairs.

Back in her room, Alisa found both the professor and Douglas sitting in the same disconsolate manner she had observed as she'd left.

'Right!' she announced briskly, marching in and going to her luggage. 'The expedition is back on. We leave in an hour.'

'Did García come?' the professor asked, jumping up with a good deal of elation on his face.

'No,' Alisa informed him steadily, 'I'm going in his place. The great leader has agreed to overlook the fact that I'm a woman.'

'You take some overlooking this morning,' Douglas remarked admiringly. 'Did you knock him down and jump on him?'

'I did not. He needed a doctor. I'm available. And by his expression I would say he thinks I'll be capable of carrying out my duties if you all stay healthy.'

'You did this for me, Alisa,' her uncle stated quietly. 'After your encounter with Lucas last night, I know it took a lot of courage to face him. Thank you, my dear.'

'I suspect that Señor Sanchez is also doing this for you,' Alisa pointed out shrewdly. 'Certainly he's prepared to cast aside his own likes and dislikes to hold this expedition together, and I don't really think he would do that just for himself.'

It was lucky that her uncle didn't know about this morning's encounter with the great leader or he would be even more impressed by her courage. She would keep that information to herself.

'However,' she finished, 'his final, sharp words were, "One hour at the latest"—so let's get moving. I'll change back into my disguise.'

'Are you glad, Al?' Douglas asked as her uncle hurried out of the room to collect his belongings.

'Time will tell,' Alisa muttered, making a wry face. 'I'll set foot on the Andes and that will be fabulous. On the other hand, I'll have to face that man every day. I can only hope he makes me walk by myself and ignores me. Anyway, Uncle Bill's happy.'

'So am I,' Douglas assured her. 'You're quite a girl.'

Quite a fool, Alisa mused as he left. In all probability she would be regretting this gesture before the day was out. She changed back into her khaki trousers and shirt, but this time she stuffed the red cap into her rucksack. Quickly plaiting her hair, she looked around the room she would not be seeing for a while and then went down to join the others. She had already arranged to leave her extra things at the hotel and she was as ready as she ever would be.

They were gathered on the steps, all their things around them, and as Alisa had expected Lucas Sanchez ignored her. This was obviously how he intended to go on. It suited her fine. Last night he had made her feel breathless and peculiar and she wanted nothing to do with him. All the same, she inspected him surreptitiously.

He might be half European, but he certainly didn't show it. The thick black hair was the sort of intense black that few Europeans could boast. It was heavy, shining and straight—only the part that curved around his forehead showing any tendency to bend at all.

The face was like carved bronze, with high cheek-bones and a strong jawline. His eyes were peculiar too, and, though their brown depths showed an English mother's blood, they were long and slightly alien-looking.

He glanced at her, his straight black brows rising questioningly, and Alisa rapidly looked away. She didn't want any attention from him and she didn't want any thunderous statements before they had even loaded up their things into the Land Rovers.

'You will travel in the lead vehicle, *señorita*,' he ordered, ignoring the fact that she had quickly turned her face away. 'Before we leave, is there anything you need?'

That startled her, and she looked up in surprise, but his face was expressionless. She hoped he was not about to make concessions to her femininity. She had never accepted that kind of concession. She was going to be a doctor, and as far as she was concerned the role was neither masculine nor feminine. And that was a fact.

'I would like to inspect the medical supplies,' she said firmly, looking him in the eye. 'I would hate to get miles away and find that some necessary thing had been left out.'

'They have been obtained on Dr García's orders,' Lucas Sanchez stated coldly. 'I assure you, *señorita*, that he is a very well qualified doctor.'

'I don't doubt it,' Alisa said quietly. 'However, every good workman checks his tools personally. If we find ourselves without some vital thing it will be my responsibility, and not much use blaming Dr García while someone suffers.'

He agreed with a slight inclination of his head and rapped out a few words to one of the men with the vehicles. It was not Spanish and Alisa assumed it was some native language. The words brought rapid action, and seconds later she was crouching down and opening the dark blue bag that was handed to her. It was neatly packed with all the things she would need unless there was some major injury, and Alisa closed it after a painstaking inspection and slung the heavy strap over her shoulder.

Lucas Sanchez snapped his fingers and the man came forward to take the bag, but Alisa shook her head.

'I'll take this,' she insisted. 'As I'm responsible for it, I'll keep it close.'

'You will take some time to get used to the thin air and the rough journey. We need your expertise, not your muscle power, *señorita*. Let the man take it.'

'I'll give it a whirl myself first,' Alisa stated inflexibly, and he shrugged his shoulders, dismissing her with a look of impatience.

'As you wish, *señorita*.' He looked round at the others. 'As we seem to be ready, I can think of no reason why we should not depart.'

'I was beginning to think this would never happen,' her uncle said happily, and Sanchez nodded.

'We can thank your niece. Let us hope she does not live to regret her generous offer.'

'It was not particularly generous,' Alisa interrupted. 'I always intended to be on this trip. The generosity is Dr García's, in being too ill to go.'

'I will pass on your compliments if we get back unscathed,' Lucas Sanchez retorted sardonically. His dark eyes flared over her and she stiffened with annoyance. She was being inspected like a schoolchild. 'You have a hat, *señorita*?' he enquired coolly.

'In my bag.' It was very difficult to be even civilised with this man. He antagonised her more than anyone had ever done in her whole life.

'Then may I suggest that you take it from your bag and put it on your head?' he said icily. 'The red cap that covered your hair last night will not in any way do either. Here we have the highest concentration of cosmic rays in the world, and they are ignored at your peril. We are going into high mountains, and though it will be cold at night, and even during the day at times, the sun is still strong and dangerous. If our doctor should have sunstroke we would be left at the mercy of all manner of catastrophes.'

'I've got a floppy hat in my bag,' Alisa flared, wanting to add much more but restraining herself. Sarcastic devil! He would push her to the very limit of endurance and she knew it.

'Then place it on your head, *señorita*,' he murmured. 'We will be greatly impressed—even if it is frilled and trimmed around the edges with lace.'

Alisa fumbled in her bag, with everyone waiting and watching her. Her face was red with embarrassment and hatred raced like hot liquid through her veins. He was trying to undermine her confidence and making her look a fool in front of everyone. Jeff Lane had obviously been told about her disguise and he was highly amused. Even the men waiting to load the luggage were watching her intently. She didn't know if they spoke any English but they had obviously got the gist of things. It was clear that she had been given a sharp dressing down.

The hat was plain white cotton, wide-brimmed and definitely floppy, and as Alisa found it and jammed it on her head with a furious disregard for fashion Sanchez nodded in ironic approval.

'*Muy bien*,' he growled. 'Now put up your collar and we will be off.'

Alisa opened her mouth to snap at him, but he turned away, ignoring her. He swung himself up into the lead vehicle, taking the wheel, and her uncle climbed into the seat beside him. The hot words died on Alisa's lips and she stood there uncertainly. When he had told her to go in the first Land Rover she had expected one of the men who had brought the vehicles to the hotel door to be driving. She had never thought that he would be driving it himself, and the last thing she wanted was to be near him.

He looked across at her and indicated the back seat. 'We are about to leave,' he reminded her drily. 'If you intend to come, now would be a good time to climb on board. Or do you intend to march resolutely behind, carrying your medical supplies?'

That had her scurrying forward quickly, and as she clambered up she noticed that Douglas was in the other Land Rover with Jeff Lane. The baggage was piled on the back seat. There was luggage piled beside her too, and obviously the two drivers were not coming. She hoped that the great leader was not keeping her close because she was a woman and likely to need help. It was much more likely, though, that he was keeping her close in case she made mischief.

Douglas grinned at her and waved. Jeff Lane winked at her and they were off. It was all that mattered. Uncle Bill had had his wishes granted, and in a way so had she. The Andes were in front of her, towering into the sky, and England seemed far away. From the quiet order of the university she was heading into a wild unknown place. The land of snow-capped mountains. The land of the condor.

She shivered with pleasure, her irritation dying as a smile touched her lips. This was something she would treasure for the rest of her life, and no unpleasant man was going to spoil it for her.

She looked up and found Lucas Sanchez observing her through the driving mirror. The dark, penetrating eyes held hers for a few seconds and she quickly composed her face, trying hard to look extremely mature and capable. When she looked again he was intent on the rough road, but his lips were twisted in a quizzical smile that didn't really bode well.

Not that she had any idea what he was thinking. He was an utterly unfathomable man—imperious as the mountains and unpredictable as a sudden storm. She hastily looked away, in case he began to observe her again, but her mind kept on probing at the subject. Why, for instance, was he so opposed to the female of the species? She knew it wasn't just her. Her uncle had told her in England that she would not be accepted.

Maybe he thought that all women were an added responsibility, or maybe he was simply hostile to her sex for personal reasons. Whatever his reasons, she was going to show him that she was as capable as a man—although she did not expect to be able to prove herself as capable as he was. There was no chance at all that he would turn out to be some weak and ineffective male. He was the most masculine being she had ever met, and the nastiest!

They soon turned off the main road and headed along another road that seemed to be curving in towards the mountains much more rapidly. The new road was rough and potholed, and as Alisa held herself tightly in, trying not to slide into the luggage, she realised why the Land Rovers were needed.

The mountains now seemed to be hovering over them, looking down on this party of puny human beings who advanced with such temerity. It was breathtaking to gaze up at the snowy peaks, so unreal in the blaze of the sunlight. The land was almost treeless, just scrub and coarse grass that offered no sign of luscious grazing, and it seemed to stretch endlessly too, because even though the mountains towered above, dwarfing everything with their splendour, it was only their size that perpetuated the idea that they were close.

'How long can we keep the vehicles?' her uncle asked, calling across the roar of the engine to Sanchez.

'Until late afternoon. It depends on our progress. We pick up the men in the foothills, and how soon we meet them depends entirely on our speed now. They will see us pass their village. They will be watching for us.'

'Not too fast, Lucas,' her uncle begged ruefully. 'It's damned uncomfortable, bouncing about like this. I'd rather be walking any time.'

'That will come soon enough. Do not anticipate it. Remember that it is some time since you climbed here. Even with your past exploits before you, you will have to acclimatise to the thin air.' He glanced in the mirror and raised his voice a little. 'And you, *señorita*? Are you also being shaken about by our less than luxurious transport?'

'Don't worry about Alisa,' her uncle said quickly. 'She may look slender, even fragile at times, but she's tough, Lucas.'

'No doubt she has impressed that fact upon you.' The dark face suddenly looked wryly amused, and Alisa was surprised to see the flash of white teeth as he grinned. Even so, she was annoyed. He was still having a go at her, even though they were flying along and bouncing about uncomfortably.

A good while later—in fact it seemed like hours later—her uncle turned to have a look at her, and Alisa quickly wiped the pained expression from her face. She was quite sure that the cold-voiced man at the wheel was aiming the car at every pothole and small boulder in the road.

'How are you doing, Alisa?' her uncle asked. 'I'm sure this will be the most uncomfortable part of the journey.'

'Do not bank on it, Professor,' Lucas Sanchez growled. He took his hand off the wheel and pointed skywards. 'We are going up there. It is not for the faint-hearted. It is pointless to soothe your niece with gentle words.'

'Oh, come on, Lucas—' her uncle began, and Alisa was surprised to hear their icy leader grunt in exasperation.

'*Por Dios*, Professor, call me Luc. Everyone else does.'

'I like to call you Lucas,' Professor Fenton protested. 'It has a good ring.'

'*Sí*! The ring of formality,' he growled. 'My father also uses my full name, with the same ancient decorum. I am often surprised that he does not address me as *señor*. I prefer to be called Luc.'

'All right,' Alisa's uncle laughed. 'Anything for a quiet life.'

'And you, *señorita*?' The dark eyes once again shot a quick look at Alisa. 'Are you prepared to concede anything for this "quiet life"?'

'Not much, Señor Sanchez,' Alisa stated unflinchingly, turning to gaze out of the window at her side. 'I can take life as it comes. I'm not really bothered about it being quiet.'

'Then I can promise you satisfaction,' Luc Sanchez assured her. 'Once we are up there in the mountains, life will be—interesting, and you will have no alternative but to take it as it comes.'

That was a threat, even though his voice seemed to be warmed by suppressed laughter, and Alisa supposed that the laughter—if there really had been any—was entirely due to his knowledge that the next few weeks would be more than she could cope with. She tightened her lips and kept silent. If it was the last thing she did, she would show this arrogant man that she was not to be treated so contemptuously. With any luck, he would be the first person to need her medical skills.

A quick, surreptitious glance at his broad shoulders made her doubt that. Only an utterly unforeseen accident would dent that tough hide. And it wasn't only that, she conceded. He was all-powerful, all-knowing—and, for all she knew, all-wise. He was the worst kind of enemy because he didn't seem to have one weakness, and she had to admit that when she looked at him, she felt less than tough as boots.

The sight of him at the hotel and since had reminded her very firmly that she was, after all, female, with normal feminine frailties. She would have to rely on her brain. Alisa stole a wary look at him again. So far, she had not found much wrong with his brain either, but it was galling even to consider that she had met her match in Luc Sanchez. Time would tell. For now, she was stuck with him.

Although they were heading into the foothills, it seemed to be taking them a very long time, and Alisa realised that not only was the closeness of the mountains merely a deception, they were approaching in a diagonal way that added distance to the journey.

The ride had not become any more comfortable, and she could even tell by the back of his neck that Uncle Bill was not appreciating it any more than she was herself. Luc Sanchez glanced in the mirror and noticed the expression on her face, and seconds later he pulled to the side of the road and stopped. The road had now become more or less a track, and when the engine died the silence was awesome.

The mountains were definitely closer, alarming in their height and power. They seemed to have life in some peculiar way, and Alisa could imagine that to primitive people they would have been a source of legend and apprehension. She felt apprehensive herself, and she gazed up at them in silence.

'Stretch your legs, *señorita*,' Luc Sanchez suggested as her uncle climbed down and stamped about and the other vehicle drew in behind them. 'This is the only stop we get, but I would not wish you to become too uncomfortable.'

'Please don't make any concessions for me,' Alisa said tightly. 'Whatever is necessary I'll do—just like everyone else.'

'I am sure you will,' he taunted. 'You will, after all, have little alternative. However, this rest is not merely for your benefit. Your uncle, too, has found the trip unpleasant. Do not feel that this stop will in any way lessen your reputation as a strong and fearless explorer. The professor has informed me that you are tough. I believe him. Certainly your ability to hold your own verbally has been proved.'

Which, being translated, meant that he considered her to be a shrew, Alisa concluded. The cynical expression on his face confirmed it. She stepped down and avoided him by making for Douglas and the other Land Rover.

'Oh, my aching bones,' Douglas muttered, grimacing at her. 'Don't tell me that Señor Sanchez is feeling the strain?'

'Not at all. This stop is for my uncle. It's not even for me—a mere female,' Alisa told him. 'The leader's name is Luc, by the way, although I'm not sure if we're permitted to address him so informally. Uncle Bill has been ordered to say Luc, when spoken to.'

'You don't like him much, do you, Al?' Douglas laughed, and Alisa pulled a wry face.

'I didn't realise you were given to making understatements,' she confessed drily. 'I might just be able to put up with him if he left me strictly alone, but he's not going to do that. He makes fun of me and belittles me at every opportunity.'

'Honestly?' Douglas looked at her oddly. 'I can't imagine him making fun in any way at all. I wouldn't have thought there was much fun in him.'

'Oh, it's all cruelty orientated,' Alisa assured him. 'Not your normal, jolly type of fun. I would imagine that his idea of fun would be to shout off the distance in feet as you fell down a crevasse.'

'For Pete's sake! That's not funny either, Al! Have you looked upwards recently?'

'I have,' Alisa assured him, glancing behind her at the towering heights that made her feel slightly lost and insignificant. 'Magnificent! This is something we'll never forget.'

'Just so long as I live to remember,' Douglas remarked, turning as Jeff Lane spoke to him.

That was when Alisa felt a hand on her arm that she was not likely to forget. Even before he spoke she knew that it was Luc Sanchez, although she had not heard him approach. The previous evening had stayed in her mind, and as his hand touched her Alisa felt a flare of unease that transmitted itself to her skin like a remembered shock. It wasn't at all the feeling she had when anyone else touched her.

'It is time to continue our journey, Señorita Fenton. If you do not need a drink or anything else we will be on our way.'

'I'm fine, thank you,' Alisa assured him. She had an insane desire to close her eyes, so that she would not have to look up and meet the cold, sardonic gaze. Her stubborn character surfaced, however, and she met the dark gaze unflinchingly. 'How long will it be before we leave the Land Rovers and proceed on foot?'

'About two hours.' He turned back towards her uncle and Alisa found herself walking beside him in an almost normal manner. 'Had we gone in a straight line to the mountains, following the main road, we would have been there much sooner. However, we are not heading where others usually go. We have been cutting across country for some time. That is why the road is so rough. The bouncing about is unavoidable.'

'I'm not complaining,' Alisa pointed out quietly. 'I expected things to be reasonably uncomfortable. I don't suppose I had even imagined a road.'

'The professor did not brief you on this? He did not explain the expedition?' Luc asked, looking down at her in some surprise.

'He never really intended that I should be here,' Alisa confessed. 'All the time before we came was taken up in arguing. I was determined to come and he was equally determined to leave me behind.'

'But you won all the same, *señorita*.'

'Only because Dr García was ill. My uncle knew quite well that you would see through my disguise, and he never told me that you'd seen the photograph. He just let me carry on forcefully, knowing quite well that it would all come to nothing.'

'You are angry with your uncle?' Luc Sanchez asked softly, and Alisa found herself smiling at the impossibility of that.

'I'm never angry with him for more than a few minutes. I care about him too much for that. All the same, he was very deceitful.'

'And so were you, *señorita*,' Luc Sanchez pointed out quietly.

'Not that it did me much good,' Alisa reminded him, and she was surprised to see a reminiscent smile tilt his lips.

'Even without the photograph, you truly imagined I would think you were a man?'

'I thought there was an even chance I would get away with it. Anyway—' Alisa sighed '—that's why I knew nothing about this, other than the things Uncle Bill told me when I was a child.'

'Then let us hope that before this is over you have more than childhood memories of South America.'

'I already have,' Alisa muttered, thinking of his overpowering and dominating personality.

'I will assume that you mean the sight of the Andes, *señorita*,' he murmured wryly. They came to the Land Rover and he politely handed her in to her seat. 'When we are camped for the night, you must tell me about your medical training,' he finished silkily. 'It is as well to know what sort of a doctor we are relying on.'

'I told you I was just learning,' Alisa said quickly, giving him an anxious look. 'If you're expecting me to perform an operation you'd better drop me here and hope for the best.'

He looked up at her with ironic satisfaction.

'I doubt if an operation will be necessary. I would imagine that first aid will do nicely. As to dropping you here, how do you think you would make your way back? The vehicle may be uncomfortable, but it is more swift than walking and not nearly so lonely.'

With this unsettling statement he got behind the wheel and ignored her, and Alisa pondered on how easily he could upset her, even when he was being what she supposed was pleasant—for him! Her uncle came back, and after asking how she was he settled into his seat happily. The short break had refreshed him more than she had expected. Alisa did not feel refreshed at all but she knew that it was nothing to do with the break. It was Luc Sanchez.

After that there was no stopping, and as the afternoon approached they began to climb slowly. They had reached the foothills, and before long Alisa knew that the ride would soon be over. From here the journey would be on foot, and as far as she could see it was going to be upwards all the way.

Now the mountains dominated completely. The sun was hot and strong, and she was thankful for the protection of the hat. Without any reminder she turned her collar up more firmly, and after that it was simply a case of waiting until Luc stopped and ordered them out. She had to admit that by now the thrill of the Andes was somewhat overshadowed by their power, by the feeling they gave her that she was insignificant.

She looked towards the driving mirror and Luc's dark eyes were on her, noting her expression. His face was quite still, with none of the sardonic amusement she had seen before, and as they stopped he sat for a moment, staring at her unwaveringly. When he got down he came round to her and insisted on helping her out.

'Some people,' he said quietly, 'are unnaturally intimidated by mountains. They are mighty, overwhelming and give the sense that mere humans are nothing, unworthy of survival. Some people succumb to this phobia. Do not be drawn into the trap, *señorita*. Magnificent they may be, and awesome, beautiful and remote, but they are merely rock. *You* can think. They cannot. Remember that.'

For a few seconds the dark eyes held hers, and Alisa took a long, shuddering breath. Tension seemed to ooze away and she managed a slight smile.

'Thank you,' she said, almost in a whisper. He had somehow read her fears and dispelled them—pushing them, at the very least, to the back of her mind.

'De nada, señorita,' he assured her quietly. 'Guard your wandering thoughts until you are used to both the thin air and the high mountains. Remember that you are not a gullible peasant. You are civilised—almost a doctor.'

His lips twisted ironically and then he turned and left her, and Alisa stared after him with almost the same awe on her face that had been there when she had begun to fear the mountains. Sometimes he seemed to be almost uncivilised himself, even though she recognised the wealth and the authority that sat so easily on him. But there was an uncanny way about him, and he seemed to be able to pick up her thoughts as if she had spoken aloud.

CHAPTER FOUR

THE Land Rovers were drawn up close together on flat land between two spurs of rock, and as far as Alisa could see there was no sign at all of the porters who were supposed to meet them. If he was annoyed at such tardiness Luc gave no sign, and she was very pleased when he organised a small fire and began the preparations for a meal.

Cooking utensils were unearthed from the vehicles, and very soon the smell of food being cooked wafted to her nostrils. It was fresh meat and Alisa wondered what it was. On the way they had passed small villages where herds of sheep and llamas had grazed on the sparse grasses, and she assumed that the meat must be either some form of mutton or the flesh of the llamas. Whatever it was, the aroma was appetising, and she realised that none of them had eaten since breakfast.

Being female, her conscience soon began to trouble her when she noted that Luc and Jeff Lane were doing most of the work. The professor was sitting with maps, his spectacles on the end of his nose, and Douglas seemed to be doing more harm than good, wandering around the fire and talking to anyone who would listen.

Alisa hauled herself stiffly to her feet and approached Luc Sanchez as he squatted by the fire wielding a huge frying pan, frequently tossing succulent pieces of meat.

'What can I do?' she enquired, and he squinted up at her through the smoke.

'Nothing, *señorita*. You are not at all acclimatised. This is simply a small meal to keep us going until nightfall. Normally the porters will cook for us. They are very good at organising the meals. Tonight we will set up camp and eat properly.' He nodded to a strong metal jug that nestled in the hot embers of the fire. 'Pour yourself a mug of coffee and sit down. Rest your back and your conscience. Forget that you are a woman. Here we are all equal.'

He gave her a long, dark, sideways glance, and Alisa was surprised to see amusement glittering in the depths of his eyes. At the moment she did not feel equal to anything, but he seemed to be filled with boundless energy, his hair black as night and his skin like polished bronze.

'I think some of us are more equal than others,' she muttered, reaching for the pot. He gave a low chuckle and tossed her a thick cloth.

'It is hot,' he warned. 'Even the most equal of us can be burned.' She took his point. She had just been about to touch a handle that had been almost directly in the flames. At this rate she would be needing her own services as the expedition's doctor before anyone else.

The coffee was strong and hot and she spooned dark sugar into it and then went back to her seat by the rocks. She was too tired really to feel much guilt; in fact she felt quite sleepy and rather breathless.

'The altitude.' Her uncle joined her and gave her a searching glance. 'It will pass quite quickly. It doesn't take much to get used to. Just take it easy for a while.'

'Doesn't he feel like this?' Alisa asked quite fretfully, her eyes on Luc's dark face and capable, busy hands.

'Nothing much affects him,' her uncle assured her, his gaze following hers. 'I've known him for a long time and he always manages to astonish me. It's a much more reasonable climate where he lives, but he comes in and out of the Andes with no apparent problems. He seems to be able to do everything—at least, I've never found him out if he can't. The map I've been looking at is Luc's. He drew it from aerial photographs. And who do you think was flying the plane?'

'Señor Sanchez,' Alisa presumed rather glumly, and her uncle nodded.

'As I say, I can't think of much he doesn't do.'

At the moment he had produced a simple meal. Douglas was standing by as waiter as Luc dished it out and Jeff Lane handed out bread which he had cut into thick slabs.

'Primitive, but it will fill us until nightfall,' Luc announced. He brought his meal and sat on the rock slightly above Alisa, looking down at her a trifle ironically as she eyed her meat and the thick, coarse bread. 'Corn bread and llama, Señorita Fenton. Eat it. You will then feel better.'

Alisa would not have dared to refuse. She had no desire to give him the chance to call her a squeamish and delicate female. She had undertaken to match the rest and she set upon her meal with great determination, almost choking on the hot meat.

'*Cuidado*!' he warned softly. 'If you choke, I will have to leave you here. It would be better to take care and survive.'

'I'll survive!' Alisa looked up at him resentfully as she heard the smoothly sardonic words. 'I didn't expect so much heat.'

'There will be less when you calm down.' It was merely a casual murmur, but the way he looked down at her brought a quick flush to Alisa's cheeks. He turned to her uncle and Alisa found herself ignored as they began to discuss the route and the problems.

At least it gave her the time to cool her temper. She found the meat delicious and the corn bread filling, and, washed down with strong, sweet coffee, it seemed at that moment the best meal she had eaten in years.

It was impossible not to glance at Luc Sanchez, and as he was totally absorbed by his conversation with the professor she was able to observe him surreptitiously. Jeff Lane was also absorbed, and Douglas looked as worn out as she felt.

'Two days' climbing should bring us to the small lake,' Luc surmised, jabbing one long brown finger in the direction of the map that was spread across her uncle's knees. 'Slightly westward from that point is the road I saw.'

'Road?' Alisa couldn't help interrupting. She knew that roads spanned the Andes, many of them through passes that were often blocked by snow, but he was talking about a road actually in the mountains. 'Is it a track?'

'If I am not mistaken, it is a road—or at the very least the remains of one,' Luc Sanchez assured her. 'The roads built by the Incas are unmistakable. They are twenty-four feet wide and mostly stone-based.'

'Stone-based?' Alisa repeated in astonishment, and he looked down at her quizzically.

'You will have observed, *señorita*, that there is a lot of stone. Surely it is not surprising that they used it?'

'Somehow,' Alisa muttered, 'I wouldn't have thought they would be bothered.'

She was surprised to see a grin come to Luc's face.

'They were not as tired as you are at this moment. Besides, they had plenty of labour and no option was given. The roads were planned and then each community built to the edge of its own boundary. No doubt many died in the attempt, but what was left behind was a network of roads that can only be compared with the Roman roads. The Incas built ten thousand miles of all-weather highway. One road ran down the coast through Peru, and the Royal road stretched from the edge of the kingdom through Ecuador, Peru, Bolivia and into Argentina and Chile. The Royal road was three thousand two hundred and fifty miles long—longer than any Roman road. The empire was held together by this system of communication.'

'But what about the one you saw in the mountains?' Alisa asked earnestly, her eyes on his strong, lean face. 'I—I mean . . . that's up in the air in a way.'

'There were lateral roads from almost every valley, bridged over water where necessary. How high they went we do not exactly know, but I am assuming that if there was any sort of place of importance—for worship or mining—then a road would be produced to reach it. What I saw from the air may be the last remaining part of such a road. Let us hope so. We are more or less banking on it.'

Listening to him had been absorbing, and Alisa realised that an odd excitement had now entered her mind. Suddenly the history of the place was more alive. It was not just the beauty and awesomeness of the mountains, not just a desire to see what her uncle had seen for so many years. She felt a faint quiver of the same feeling that the professor and Luc felt. The excitement of the chase. Not the hunting of some creature but the race to capture the past.

'I would estimate that your meat is now quite cool enough to be tackled in safety,' Luc Sanchez murmured, and she suddenly became aware that since he had stopped speaking she had been staring at him in fascination, absorbing his words, dreaming about the past and just looking at him intently.

Her face flushed slightly and she ducked her head and applied herself once more to the meal.

'Thank you for telling me all that,' she said breathlessly. 'It's made it all real. I—I expect all the others know about it already.'

'*Desde luego*. They are either scholars or enlightened amateurs. They are here because this is their kind of life. They are not here to protect an uncle from his own folly.'

Alisa's head shot up, sparks flying from her blue eyes, but he had already moved and was walking with that easy, swinging stride back to the fire. He was like a powerful, ferocious animal, she thought furiously. And he had used her thanks to take a quick swipe at her, like an animal who just couldn't resist a slash at the enemy. It was brought home to her very sharply that relaxing into friendliness with Luc Sanchez was simply leaving herself open to attack. No doubt his small acts of kindness since they had stopped had been to make sure that she didn't expire and leave him with a problem.

There was a flurry of sound, and from the direction of one of the last villages she had noticed a mule appear, its bridle held by a very colourful character. Three more of his kind followed, and Alisa knew that the porters had arrived. Now they would set off, and she would have to make quite sure that she did not in any way lag behind and hold up the expedition. If she did, the small portion of sarcasm that Señor Sanchez had just aimed at her would be a mere whisper to be remembered with affection. If she held them up he would have no hesitation in blasting her in front of everyone.

The porters were much smaller men than any of the others present. Luc dwarfed them, and even her uncle who was not in any way a tall man was easily taller than they were. Their hair was jet-black and the oriental-looking eyes and dark faces told her at once that they were Indians—Bolivians with an ancient past, the descendants of the Incas.

They were all wearing thick, brightly coloured shirts and dark trousers, and she was not surprised to see heavy, brilliantly coloured garments draped over the mule. They were very much like the serapes worn by Mexicans, and Alisa knew that these thick, shawl-like cloaks would soon be needed. It was already beginning to get colder and she had seen the Indians close to the hotel wearing them, with the women draped in similar thick blankets, their peculiar stove-pipe hats on their dark heads.

Luc greeted them in their own language, which the professor had told her was Aymara. Either Aymara or Quechua, the language of the Incas, was spoken by most Indians, although she knew that the upper classes spoke Spanish—the language of their own ancestors. It meant that she would not be able to speak to the porters because, although she had a smattering of Spanish, the Indian languages sounded too complicated even to consider learning. Once again she would be at the mercy of Luc Sanchez, who seemed to speak every language fluently.

There was a great deal of animated discussion, and Alisa was astounded when her uncle joined in. So did Jeff Lane, and it was brought home to her that she was extremely insignificant. Even Douglas was involved, because he seemed to be taking notes as everyone spoke, and she had no doubt that he was getting words down fast. Before they went back he would know something of the Aymara tongue. All she would have was a sore back and the opportunity to do a bit of first aid.

'Do not look so downcast, Señorita Fenton,' a dark voice advised, and Alisa looked up to find Luc towering over her and regarding her intently. 'You will not be left out of things. And it may be some consolation to know that Chano speaks English.'

It was becoming quite alarming, this way he had of picking up her thoughts, and Alisa looked up at him warily.

'Which one is Chano?'

Luc pointed to a quite merry-looking Indian who was busily organising the others, and, catching her eye, the small, energetic-looking man nodded pleasantly. That was a relief. At least she wouldn't be surrounded by hostile people. Although, thinking about it, the only hostility she had faced had been from Luc Sanchez. He was so overwhelming, though, that his attitude set the tone.

The Land Rovers were unpacked and most of the supplies were loaded onto the mule, with the rest as packs for the Indians to carry. The others carried their own small personal packs, and as Alisa adjusted hers and reached for the medical bag she found her hand arrested by strong brown fingers.

'Let it go,' Luc said quietly. 'The terrain is rough, the air thin. Nothing will happen to the supplies, and if by any chance we lose them I will be responsible.'

Alisa opened her mouth to argue. It seemed to be the natural thing to do with him, but as she looked up she changed her mind. For once, he was not looking superior or sarcastic. There was a softening of his expression, a look of quiet understanding that stilled her tongue.

'You will not be backing down,' he continued with an amused look at her changing expression. 'This is an expedition, not a battle. Until I am sure that you are going to be perfectly safe, I would like to be certain that you have both hands free. For the rest of the day you are going to find this trip tiring. Let Chano take the supplies. He is reliable.'

'All right.' Alisa put the strap of the bag into Luc's hand, meeting his enigmatic gaze with as much courage as she could muster. 'I'll try not to battle. It's second nature, though.'

'Unnecessary here,' Luc assured her. 'You are not under attack. And remember, *señorita*, I *asked* you to join us finally. Without you, this trip would not be taking place.'

It was a startling admission and Alisa looked at him suspiciously, but he seemed to be perfectly serious and she took a long, steadying breath.

'Thank you for—for saying that,' she said quietly. 'I still feel as if I've forced my way into this.'

'You have not,' he assured her flatly. Lean brown fingers curved round her chin and tilted it, making her meet his dark eyes. 'I would not have allowed it. Nobody forces their way into anything that I control. I needed you. It is that simple.'

He walked off, taking the medical bag to Chano, and Alisa stared after him uneasily. It was very worrying when his fingers touched her skin. Not exactly pleasant, but worrying all the same. She had felt like that from the moment in the hotel garden, and now her heart was beating heavily, uncomfortably. It was the thin air, she decided, ignoring the fact that she had been perfectly all right before he had come near her.

'What's going to happen to the Land Rovers?' Alisa asked the professor as he came up to her just before they set off. 'Are they just being left here?'

'No. They would be quite safe, but later on someone will come from Chano's village and drive them back there. When we come down they'll be here waiting for us. They know more or less when we're due and they'll just wait. Patience is one of their characteristics.'

Patience was not one of Luc's characteristics. There was no doubt about that, and she wondered how he would react if the vehicles were not there when they returned. At least it would be interesting—providing she had nothing to do with it!

It was easy climbing at first, because there was a rough track that wound its way between rocks. Alisa decided to ignore the mountains and their rather frightening height. If she looked up they overwhelmed her, their strength and inevitability shattering her self-confidence, so she looked no further than was necessary.

They proceeded in single file. In front of her was Douglas, who followed her uncle, and at the head of the file Luc, with Chano behind him. Jeff Lane followed Alisa and then the other porters, one of them bringing the mule. Any angry thoughts she had had previously of being sent to the back and made to lag behind were forgotten. Luc had arranged the walking order and she knew that she was tucked in safely. Ordinarily that would have annoyed her, but now it only made her feel more secure.

When the track ended they went diagonally, climbing the rock-strewn terrain, always moving upwards, closer to the snow-capped peaks that seemed to be now much more distant. There was still warmth in the sun but before they had started all of them had put on sweaters, and, although Alisa found the going strenuous because of the thin air, she was not too hot. Up here the wind that blew constantly over the plain was, oddly enough, not so strong, sheltered as they were by rocky outcrops and folds in the mountains. She knew, however, that when the sun finally set the cold would be unavoidable.

Two hours later they came to a flat stretch of land that was well sheltered and even had a growth of coarse grasses and small struggling bushes, and here Luc called a halt. It was getting late. Soon the sun would set behind the mountains, and this was their first camp. It was a shallow, rocky basin and Alisa was glad to see it. She doubted if she could have gone on for much longer and she was greatly relieved to see that Douglas was in a similar state. It was not just her feminine physique, because Douglas was no weakling.

They all dropped their packs and she looked round for her uncle.

'How do you feel?' she asked anxiously as she saw him leaning against a rock.

'Like I always feel on the first day,' he assured her with a grin. 'Tomorrow will be different. Overnight I'll acclimatise, and I imagine you will too.'

'I have to admit that I feel worse than you look,' Alisa muttered ruefully, and he laughed as he put his arm round her shoulders and gave her a squeeze.

'If nothing else comes of this, it will have been worth it to stop you being anxious about me,' he assured her. 'I'm pretty tough, Alisa.'

'I know,' she sighed. '*I'm* pretty foolish, and I can see that now.'

'Oh, I don't know,' he said quizzically. 'It's good to have somebody caring. Makes me feel important.'

'A wife would have done that,' Alisa pointed out sneakily, and he pulled a wry face.

'A wife would have made me sit at my desk and give boring lectures. I would probably be retired by now and growing roses in some suburban garden. Can you see me doing that?'

'Not really.' Alisa shook her head and laughed up at him. 'I have to admit that you look more at home here.'

'There you are, then,' he pronounced happily. 'This trip has ironed out our difficulties.'

'It may have ironed out yours, but I rather think that mine are facing me,' Alisa said a trifle grimly, her eyes on the darkening mountains. The sun was going down and shadows were coming fast across the lower slopes. Behind the high peaks the setting sun was a brilliant gold, and the moving shadows were dark blue, purple and black as they rushed into the caves and crevices of the rocky landscape.

'Tomorrow you'll wake up filled with energy and the desire to conquer,' the professor promised her, but Alisa's eyes fell on the dark figure of Luc Sanchez and she knew that the word conquer did not fit her at all, not when he was near. He was organising the camp as if he had never even walked at all. The tiredness that the others were showing did not seem to have touched him. He was as used to this land as the Indians whose ancestors had faced the Incas and been absorbed by their culture, and the language that drifted across to her as he gave out orders to the small, lively men who had joined them with the mule was as alien as Luc's dark eyes.

Before night fell there was a roaring fire in the shelter of the rocks. The tents had been pitched and Chano had organised a meal. It was some sort of stew, and Alisa had no idea what had been tossed into the ample pot but it smelled good—even though she was not feeling quite up to eating. All she could manage was a very small helping, and it was the thick, dark coffee that was most welcome. By the time darkness was complete, the camp had a lived-in air about it, as though they had been there for days.

Alisa sat by the rocks, resting back against her pack, her eyes beginning to close sleepily, and she was startled into complete wakefulness as soft, mournful music drifted through the quiet air. She knew what it was, of course. Her uncle had lots of music like that, the music of the Andes, but she had never expected to hear it so far from any village.

Across the fire the Indians were playing, their faces intent as they blew into the pipes that made the strange almost eerie sounds. She glanced across at her uncle who was sitting beside her, but he was smiling to himself, listening, his eyes half closed, and Alisa looked round sharply as someone came to sit at the other side of her.

It was Luc, but he said nothing. He didn't even glance at her, and before long she almost forgot that he was there. The music was so in keeping with the landscape, with the awe-inspiring grandeur of the mountains, that it almost seemed to be coming from somewhere else, some place that was not really for mortals.

The insidious notes seemed to creep into her soul, and finally Alisa shivered at the feeling that was coming over her. She looked across at Luc and his eyes were intently on her. His dark glance roamed over her face as the fire-light lit up the pale glow of her skin and then he looked away, calling across the flames to the Indians. She didn't know what he said but they stopped playing and all looked at her and then put their heads together for a quick discussion.

'What did he say?' Alisa whispered, leaning towards her uncle, who was regarding her with amusement.

'He asked them to play something a little more lively for the *señorita*. He told them that you are not yet used to the mountains and they are frightening you with their ghosts.'

'Is that what it was about?' Alisa asked, slightly unnerved.

'No, but it sounded a bit like that, didn't it?' The professor looked amused and Alisa nodded. At any moment she had expected fierce and ferocious conquistadors to burst in on the scene. It had been quite disconcerting, as if the whole place was waiting for the past to catch it. In spite of her anxiety at his odd skill at reading her mind, she was quite grateful to Luc.

The music began again, but this time brilliant notes rose into the air, fast and carefree, warbling and soaring up into the peaks, and all feelings of either tiredness or awe left Alisa as she sat forward and listened raptly. Chano was taking the lead while the others accompanied him, his fingers flying over the small pipe he held so easily. It was a virtuoso performance fit for any concert hall, a tune to lift the spirits, and Alisa couldn't help glancing at Luc as it ended—just as she couldn't help clapping enthusiastically.

Luc was watching her out of his eye corners, his dark eyes amused, glittering in the firelight.

'That pleased you,' he concluded, his lips quirking at her expression.

'It was wonderful!' Alisa stated, her face alight with pleasure. 'They're so good! I thought all these things were done by professional musicians. My uncle has lots of tapes of that sort of music but I never thought it was just ordinary people from the villages.'

'Mostly the musicians you hear are professionals,' he assured her. 'But these people make their own entertainment. They even make their own instruments. There is often nothing else to do.'

'It was—inspired,' Alisa mused aloud. 'It was like a sort of offering to the sky.'

'You are clever, Señorita Fenton,' Luc admitted with a slow smile. 'It is a tune from Paraguay. It is called "Los Pájaros"—the birds—and I suppose that the birds do offer their thanks to the sky. It has put a smile on your face and dispelled the gloom and they are delighted at your appreciation. You seem to have gained four devotees. They will not let you become lost.'

A quick glance told Alisa that the Indians were indeed pleased at her appreciation, and they grinned at her as she looked, their white teeth flashing in the firelight.

She smiled back a little uneasily and only realised that she had edged closer to Luc Sanchez when he said softly, 'They are not to be feared. They are very civilised, as your uncle pointed out before you came to my country, according to the small lecture you gave me in the hotel garden. They know that you admired the skill they showed and for them it will make the whole thing exciting. It is rather like a performance at the Albert Hall. An English *señorita* has applauded them. What more could they want?'

'I thought they were wonderful,' Alisa assured him sharply, moving away again and wondering how she had ever come to be talking to him in the first place. 'Do you always spoil everything with your cynical remarks?'

'But I imagined that I had given you pleasure and dispelled your anxieties,' Luc said with taunting astonishment. 'I have also assured you of your complete safety. I am to be chastised for this?'

'Oh! It's—it's just a way you have. I'm sorry,' Alisa muttered, trapped into thinking that she had been unfair. She knew that she was always going to be defensive when he was near, and he had seen how she felt and acted on her behalf.

'Do you play the pipes?' she suddenly asked, after a quick search for a change of subject.

'I do not, *señorita*,' Luc murmured drily, getting to his feet and looking at her mockingly. 'If I wish to serenade you I will whistle, but do not listen too carefully. It is unlikely to happen.'

'Pig!' Alisa muttered under her breath as he strode away and began to issue more orders. He had the ability to get under her skin as nobody else had ever done and he had her constantly off balance. He had ordered a change of atmosphere because he had seen what the other tunes were doing to her and he knew her feeling of frightened awe of the mountains. When she had tried to be normal, though, he had taken another slash at her with the power and timing of a jaguar.

'Pig!' she muttered again, and then got to her feet, ready as she had never been in her life to get to sleep.

She looked down at her uncle, but he had not fallen asleep as she had suspected. He was grinning all over his face.

'Don't let Luc hear your opinion of him,' he warned. 'I'm not sure what he would do.'

'I suspect he would hit me,' Alisa muttered scornfully, and got herself a quizzical look from the professor.

'Luc is a gentleman, and much more likely to give anything to protect you,' he assured her. 'He may be tempted to put you across his knee and spank you, though.'

'Let him dare!' Alisa said hotly, and got herself another quizzical look.

'Oh, he would dare—and I can't think of anyone here who could stop him, can you, my dear?'

'You're on his side!' Alisa declared heatedly, and he struggled to his feet, bending over to kiss her cheek.

'I'm always on your side,' he laughed. 'Luc is not used to anyone like you, though. His idea of a woman is some simpering female who sits and looks beautiful. You're a challenge, and he's not likely to ignore a challenge. Just watch your tongue, that's all I'm saying.'

'I'll be more likely to have to watch my step,' Alisa murmured with a glance at the mountains.

'Every man here will be watching your step,' her uncle assured her. 'Now you've got four more who'll do the same.'

He nodded towards the Indians, who were still staring at Alisa with smiling pleasure, and she gravely acknowledged their presence with a slight smile and an inclination of her head.

'Bravo,' her uncle laughed. 'Now that would please Luc—calm and dignified as a woman of his own circle.'

'You mean, rich, beautiful and insipid?' Alisa asked with ill-concealed scorn, and her uncle chuckled as he went off to his tent.

'I believe they're very passionate.'

His parting shot had Alisa marching to her own tent and crawling inside to her sleeping bag. Passionate! Imagine being passionate with a man like Luc Sanchez! It would be like inviting a jungle cat to stroke your face.

She suddenly had an unnerving picture of those powerful arms round her, of that dark face close to hers, and she shot into her bag as soon as her clothes were off, closing her eyes determinedly. It was certainly the thin air. She was going to be a doctor—logical, methodical and reliable. She was not given to daydreams, especially worrying ones.

She thrust the pictures of him out of her mind, and the last thought she had was that this was the only time she had ever been to bed without first taking a shower. She hadn't even washed her face. In the morning she would have to make some arrangement about that. It was another thing she had never even thought about.

CHAPTER FIVE

NEXT morning, Alisa awoke to the sounds of the camp stirring around her. It was very early, but already strong sunlight was filtering in through the partly open flap of her tent. As she noticed this Alisa became alert. She had definitely closed that flap the night before, but now it was partly unzipped. It could only mean that someone had either tried to come in or had actually been in while she slept.

Her momentary panic was stopped as she noticed a bowl of warm water just inside the tent. It was obviously for washing and she felt a wave of pleased surprise. Her uncle had slid the bowl into her tent. How thoughtful of him. It would be a hard task to get a top-to-toe wash with the amount of water, but she had never expected such a treat.

She crawled over to get it and then dived into her pack for the necessary soap and cloth. Normally she would have used about twice as much water simply to wash her hands, but this was luxury in the mountains. She was hard pressed not to break into song.

Later, spruced up, feeling fresh and hungry, Alisa ventured forth and pounced on the professor as soon as she saw him.

'Thanks for the water. It was a lovely surprise to have warm water for a wash.' She beamed at him and got a very quizzical look in reply.

'Is that sarcasm or has the thin air affected you?' he asked wryly.

'Didn't you put a bowl of warm water in my tent?' Alisa asked, although she could see that he had not by the expression on his face.

'Probably your boyfriend,' her uncle surmised with a grin. 'Sorry, Alisa, but I'm not given to quixotic gestures when I'm on a trip in the Andes.'

She could understand that, and after striking out with her uncle, Alisa approached Douglas more cautiously. He was not guilty either, but he imagined that he knew who was.

'Look at Chano,' he murmured. 'He's grinning all over his face and waiting to catch your eye. You've either got an ardent admirer there or the warm water was a payment for your wild applause last night.'

It was true. Chano was beaming at her from the other side of the camp and Alisa found her problem solved easily. She gave him a warm smile and limited her thanks to that. She did not want an ardent admirer. She wasn't sure if she wanted him poking his head into her tent either. Life was going to be difficult enough as it was.

That fact was brought home to her as she saw Luc issuing serious orders to the men, and in a few minutes he was joining them and advising everyone to eat, pack and be ready to leave forthwith. Sleeping had not softened him, Alisa noted with a frown. He was still tall, powerful and unbending. It was hard to imagine that last night she had had ridiculous fantasies about being held in those sun-bronzed arms. First night in the Andes, no doubt. Disorientation. The odd feelings had left her this morning.

Luc glanced at her hair, which was still hanging loosely over her shoulders, the sunlight turning it to gold, and she saw the error of her ways at once under the frowningly intent gaze. She was being normal, feminine and a pest. She turned away and began to plait her hair with some haste, and it was only later that she realised how he had got her anxious without saying a single word.

She glared at him, found her hat and jammed it on her head, although the sun was by no means hot as yet. In fact it was very cold now, even in the sunlight, and she was glad of the sweater and jacket she had put on as soon as she was up. Luc met her angry looks with total uninterest, and Alisa wondered if she had also imagined his amused kindness the night before, when he had requested another tune to cheer her up.

Later, as they continued their steady climb, it slowly dawned on her that she was already acclimatised. As her uncle had surmised, the effects of the thin air had vanished overnight, and she did not feel either worn out or sleepy. In fact, she felt full of energy and decidedly perky—a state of mind that Luc observed with one of his flashing glances and evidently did not find encouraging. He scowled at her and continued on his way. Alisa pulled a face at him, but not until he had turned his head. The boss-man looked very irritable this morning, she mused. Somebody was sure to suffer and she had to make quite sure that it was not going to be her.

The going was decidedly more difficult than the day before, and Alisa was thankful for the strong climbing boots that covered her feet. As the day progressed she discarded her jacket, tying it around her waist, and she was very glad that Luc had persuaded her to give the medical supplies to Chano. It was more than enough to carry her own pack.

So far she had not needed to use her hands to help her along at all, because although they were climbing upwards there was no actual rock-climbing as she had imagined. The mountains continued to dominate her thinking, to remind her of her puny state, and several times she had recourse to consider Luc's advice. She could think. They could not.

Gradually, this philosophy sank in and she relaxed, even beginning to feel part of the whole expedition for the first time, but her relaxed frame of mind was shaken badly as they stepped out onto the edge of a deep gorge, a thing that took her completely by surprise. They seemed to be standing on the top of the world, and for a long time all of them gazed at the high peaks and then down the sheer drop that lay before them.

The depth seemed to be endless, although it was possible to see, very far below, the rock-strewn floor of the gorge. Tough-looking bushes grew up the sides, clinging tenaciously to the rocky walls, and Alisa was glad that she did not suffer from vertigo—because they were all merely minute dots on the vast landscape.

'We cross here,' Luc said firmly, and it was only then that Alisa turned her head and saw the bridge.

It was slung across the gorge from one side to the other, the sort of thing she had seen in adventure films, and she stared at it in horror. Stone structures at each side held the suspension cables of thick, twisted rope, and the floor of the bridge was wooden planking as far as she could see. The whole thing dipped low in the middle, sagging under its own weight, and all around the mountains looked down on it coldly.

'I can't do that,' Alisa said softly, her voice shaken. Nobody was meant to hear, but she saw Luc's head turn sharply and his dark eyes held hers unwaveringly. He said nothing, and Alisa thought that perhaps he had not heard after all. It didn't matter much whether he had heard or not. She knew her own capabilities and she could never step on to that swaying, terrifying structure.

Luc waved his arm and Chano came forward, leading the mule to the bridge, but the animal balked in fright, stiffening its legs. For a second, Chano stood by its head, talking to it in a low voice. Then he led it forward, and to Alisa's amazement she could hear him singing to it in the same low voice, the strange, unearthly music of the Andes that had held her in some awe so recently.

They all watched. It was utterly compelling, and step by step the man and the animal drew away. Although their weight made the bridge sway considerably, the mule did not stop again. Whether it was the singing or Chano's steady presence, Alisa did not know. She just watched them as they crossed the frightening, swaying bridge, her eyes wide with anxiety.

It was with great relief that Alisa saw them get to the other side and step on to firm footing. She gave a deep sigh. Her legs were shaking and she had stood all the time with her hands clenched in front of her until her fingers were white with the tension. She almost cried out in panic when Luc's hand came to her shoulder.

'The mule was afraid and yet he went,' the dark voice reminded her calmly. 'With Chano and the mule on the bridge together there was much weight, but they did not fall, the bridge did not break. The mule has no hands to hold himself steady. He trusted to Chano. I will take you across. You will trust me, *señorita*?'

It dawned on her then that he had sent Chano across with the mule so that she could watch. He had done it to encourage her, and although she was still terrified she had seen them cross without injury.

'All right,' she managed breathlessly, and walked to the beginning of the bridge with him. 'Chano sang to the mule,' she reminded him with shaken humour. 'Are you going to sing to me?'

He grinned down at her, his brown fist brushing her chin in a softly teasing caress.

'If it becomes necessary. I think, however, that once on the bridge you will be filled with elation.'

'There,' Alisa muttered, 'and I was beginning to think that you never made an error of judgement. I'll be your first disappointment.' She looked up at him anxiously. 'Should we forget the whole thing? I'll camp here and wait for you all to come back.'

'You will not,' he laughed. 'You are our doctor. We need you.' He held out his hand and looked at her steadily. 'Come. Remember that like the mountains the mule cannot think things out. He had faith in Chano. Do not have less faith in me.'

Alisa put her hand in his and stepped out as he did. She had no alternative. If she couldn't face this then the whole expedition would grind to a halt, because she knew by now that Luc would not even consider leaving her behind. She suspected, too, that he would not contemplate sending her back with an escort either. How much of a responsibility she was depended on her courage now, and with a tight grip on his hand she just let her mind go blank and faced the bridge and the sheer drop below.

'The Incas built many of these structures,' he informed her as she clung to his hand and used her free hand to grip the ropes at the side. 'They were essential, as you can see, and very well made. Even now in some of these high places they are still kept intact. To tamper with them in Inca times was to invite the death penalty.'

'Is—is this how you're going to sing to me, with interesting words?' Alisa asked shakily, and she heard his low chuckle of amusement.

'Believe me, it is better than my singing ability. Had I sung to the mule he would have leapt over the side to escape the sound. Do not be afraid. Look ahead. Chano is watching with interest, and even the mule is filled with admiration.'

'There's nothing to admire,' Alisa assured him breathlessly. 'I've made an utter fool of myself. You're having to take me across like a child.'

'Oh, I do not agree. I am enjoying it. I would have had to carry a child. As it is, I have the pleasure of holding your hand.'

His hand tightened warmly around hers, and Alisa risked a quick glance at him but found that his lips were twisted in amusement. She didn't risk another look. It seemed more important to keep her eyes on Chano and the mule. They looked encouraging. They were safely across. She might just make it herself.

'Thank you for boosting up my shattered ego,' she muttered. 'I'm sure my uncle and Douglas will think we're really enjoying ourselves.'

'But I am enjoying myself. This is light entertainment, and not much of that exists up here. When you are not raging, I find you most amusing.'

'Thank you, Señor Sanchez,' Alisa said drily. 'I'll see what I can come up with next.'

'Next, we are going up there.' Luc was suddenly serious. He pointed to the high mountains. 'All you must do is be very, very careful. There are some places where nothing is going to save you but your own common sense and caution. When I think of that, I wonder why I was mad enough to bring you with us.'

'Why did you?' she asked, glancing up at him, the sheer drop below forgotten for the moment.

'I told you already. I needed you,' he reminded her, his eyes holding hers steadily. 'Had I not needed you, you would now be safely back in England, maligning me before your university friends.'

'Wrong,' Alisa stated, forcing herself to sound bright. 'I would have been grumbling about you all by myself and worrying about my uncle all alone. I finished at university just before we came out here.'

'And now what?' he asked with apparent interest.

'Now I go out and do my real training. I go into a hospital.'

'For how long.'

'Three years. That should show you how useless a doctor you have here. What you have is a student.'

'Señor Ellis says you are a brilliant student,' he remarked unexpectedly, and she looked at him in surprise.

'Really? Well, bravo, Douglas. He's always ready to put in a good word for me, but I'm quite surprised that he mentioned it.'

'I asked him about you. He was delighted to talk. I think he expected to be savaged if he did not offer detailed information,' Luc assured her sardonically.

'Yes,' Alisa mused, with sarcasm of her own, 'being powerful and scary has its compensations, I suppose.'

'For you too, *señorita*,' Luc murmured wryly. 'If I had been a weakling you would not have trusted me to bring you across the bridge, *es verdad*? Your Douglas looks as if he needs help himself.'

'He'll cope,' Alisa said loyally, and got herself a sideways look of scepticism.

'He will have to. I have no intention of talking him across. I have used up a whole week's conversation in assisting you. Here we are.'

He handed her on to firm ground and Alisa looked back, realising that for over half the way she had not even noticed where they were because he had deliberately held her attention by talking. She stared up at him and then began to laugh in genuine amusement.

'*Touché*, Señor Sanchez! You had me fooled with your wonderful conversation. For all that time I believed you had suddenly become human.'

'What is your odd saying?' he asked drily. 'Don't hold your breath?'

He raised his arm and the rest of them started to come across one behind the other, and she could then contemplate her position in the whole glorious scheme of things. Chano had brought the mule; Luc had brought her. They were more or less classed together. Alisa sat down and had a good laugh, and from the way Luc looked down at her with raised, dark brows she understood that he thought she was hysterical.

Well, what had she expected? He was Bolivian, utterly grand and aloof and decidedly tricky. He did what was necessary but only when it was necessary. And, after all, she was a woman. She had forgotten for a moment that she was an unacceptable member of the opposite sex.

Over the next two days they climbed steadily higher, traversing the mountains, negotiating the dangerous drops and skirting the higher points as easily as possible. They still had the mule, and there could be no spectacular scaling of heights with the animal. In any case, it was not necessary. It was possible to zigzag higher and higher with no other help than sure feet and a steady eye. The mule could do that too.

It was colder now at night, but the sun during the day was strong and dangerous and Alisa did not forget to take that into account. If she had forgotten, Luc would have pounced on her, because he was ever watchful. He was never friendly, though, and now when camp was made he did not ask for anything special for her. The

Indians had taken the point, however, and usually kept their evening tunes cheerful.

Each morning the warm water was there for her wash, and eventually she became almost uneasy about it. She never heard anyone bringing it to her tent, and however quick she was nobody was near when she peered out. She concluded that Chano had taken the task on as a duty, and although she was grateful she wondered anxiously what Luc would say if he found out. He didn't look as if he would allow favouritism. Everyone else washed in icy water from the small streams that trickled down the mountainsides. He would expect her to do the same.

As they approached their camping place in the evening of the fourth day there was a change in the air. Looking up, Alisa saw thick mist swirling down the mountains. It was completely obliterating everything and she felt a burst of alarm. If it came down to their level, there would be no way of seeing even those directly in front of them.

She breathed a sigh of relief when Luc called a halt and the camp was started early. The mist had wiped out the sun much more quickly than usual, and as Alisa looked upwards it seemed to be hanging over them like a grey, impenetrable blanket.

'Will it come right down?' she asked her uncle, and he shrugged unconcernedly.

'Possibly. Sometimes it reaches a level and stays there. It's quite weird, but by morning it will be gone. The sun will burn it off.'

'Suppose it doesn't?' Alisa ventured, and he gave her a reassuring smile.

'Then we'll probably stay here until it clears. Luc won't risk going on if he can't see. We should be near the lake soon. Perhaps tomorrow.'

'Then what?'

'Then we try to find the road Luc saw from the air. After that, it's in the lap of the gods.'

What a very appropriate remark, Alisa thought. The lap of the gods. Up here it was possible to imagine the gods, possible to know why the Indians of the past had worshipped so earnestly. It was also easy to understand why some of their gods were fierce.

She was glad to see the cheerful flames of the fire when it was lit, and she kept as close to it as possible. The meal was welcome too, and although it was pretty much the same as usual the cold air and the exercise had given her a very healthy appetite these past few days. She sat later with her coffee and relaxed, not altogether surprised when the Indians played more mournful tunes. Somehow the evening required it.

The mist came no lower. It hung above them with a threatening air that only served to make her feel small and insignificant again, and Alisa was glad when the others made a move to go to their tents. She was more than ready to crawl into her sleeping bag and she sincerely hoped that by morning the mist and the melancholy atmosphere would have gone, leaving the usual blue, high sky.

When the noise woke her, she had no idea of the time. It was inky black and she felt for her small torch, looking at her watch in the yellow beam of light. It was one in the morning, and although everything was now silent, she knew that it was no dream that had awoken her from a sound sleep.

Alisa turned the beam of light on the flap of her tent, but it was securely closed and she tried to go back to sleep. That was when she heard it again, this time quite distinctly. It was a slow trickle of sound and she could not tell whether it was close or far away. It was disturbing enough to keep her head from the pillow, though, and finally she knew that she would have to investigate.

She pulled on her clothes and crawled from the tent, greatly surprised at the scene that met her eyes. When she had gone to bed, the mist had been covering the sky, an alarming, depressing sight that had sent her scurrying to her tent readily. Now it was gone, as silently and as easily as it had come. The sky was clear and the moon was unbelievably bright, soaring in the heavens like a silver ball.

Alisa stood upright as she came from her tent, and for a second she forgot the slight insidious sound. The moon held her gaze to the exclusion of everything else. The beauty of the mountain night was curiously touching, and it was only as she heard another noise that she came to attention and thought of danger.

'What are you doing?' The cool voice of Luc Sanchez was almost in her ear, and she spun round guiltily, as if she had indeed been about to commit some crime.

'I—I heard a noise—' she began uncertainly, and found his dark eyes holding hers with cynical disbelief.

'Perhaps it was Señor Ellis telling you that everyone else was asleep?' he suggested nastily.

'What exactly do you mean by that?' Alisa demanded angrily. 'If you're suggesting that I—!'

'I am not suggesting anything,' he insisted harshly. 'I am assuming that you are out of your bed for a good reason. The reason is strong enough to bring you into the moonlight when everyone else is asleep. I conclude, therefore, that you are lonely.'

'You can damned well conclude what you like!' Alisa snapped, her eyes flashing with annoyance. 'I heard a noise, whether you believe me or not. It sounded like somebody moving stealthily about, but I couldn't tell whether it was close or far away.' She glared up at him in the moonlight. 'It was probably you, going round to see that everyone keeps out of mischief and obeys your orders!'

His hand shot out and captured her arm, but what he would have said Alisa never found out, because the noise came again—and this time she could tell that it was not in the camp.

'That's it!' she exclaimed anxiously. Right at that moment she was glad he was here, even glad of the strong grip on her arm. He had heard it too, and his grip relaxed to an easy clasp. 'Is it an animal?' she wanted to know, turning wide and worried eyes on him. 'Does anything creep about up here?'

'Only you.' He was suddenly smiling and his face turned to the mountains as he released her arm and listened, watching the slopes. 'I would be almost certain that it is a slight rock fall. Anything of major proportions and we would be in no doubt. From time to time the mountains move, turn in their sleep. Then the rocks shower down. Some of them are only loosely attached to their moorings.'

As far as she could see he was taking a very calm attitude about this and Alisa moved closer; this time she was the one to reach out, and her hand came to his arm anxiously.

'It's very picturesque and wonderfully mystical to know that the mountains turn in their sleep,' she assured him urgently, 'but I wouldn't like it one bit if they turned over on to me. How do you know that this rock fall isn't coming our way?'

'Because it is at least ten miles away,' he pointed out smoothly. 'I would not permit a camp where we could be engulfed by an avalanche of rocks. It is safe to sleep.'

'I surely hope so,' Alisa muttered, her eyes still on the mountains. She had forgotten her grip on his arm and he released her fingers, uncurling them from his skin and looking down at her. He made no attempt to release her hand, though, and Alisa found her face flushing in the bright moonlight.

'Well, now you know why I was out of my tent,' she said sharply, going onto the attack to get herself out of this situation. 'You can apologise in the morning for your remarks about Douglas.'

They were alone, as they had been in the garden of the hotel, and she was frighteningly aware of the hard strength of the body so close to her own. His eyes never left her face and she was too bewildered to look away. There was an almost hypnotic power to those dark eyes. They held hers unwaveringly, and when she tried stealthily to move her hand from his he simply tightened his grip but said nothing at all.

'Why—why were you walking about?' she asked almost frantically. It was alarming the way he didn't speak, but just looked at her and held tightly to her hand. The odd tingles were back inside, running up her arm, making her mouth dry.

'I heard you come out of your tent. I did not even bother to dress properly.' He flicked his jacket open and she could see that he was just wearing the khaki trousers he wore each day, his long boots and the jacket. Beneath the jacket his chest was bare, and the moonlight showed a strong covering of dark hair that arrowed downwards. He smelled warm, clean and masculine, and Alisa found it hard to breathe properly. She had never been so close to a man like Luc before, and the air seemed to be electric between them.

'You—you thought I was an intruder?' she ventured shakily, licking at her dry lips, but he shook his head, his eyes still watching her intently, following the unconsciously sensual movement of her tongue.

'I knew it was you. The sound came from the direction of your tent. I have excellent hearing. I did not wish to take the risk that you would wander away.'

'I wasn't walking in my sleep,' Alisa began, and his mouth twisted in a cynical smile.

'I wondered if you were lonely and heading for the tent of your boyfriend. It would not be good for morale.'

'Douglas is not my boyfriend,' she managed unevenly. 'We're just friends—college friends.'

'*De veras*?' he enquired softly. 'Then when you go back to England and leave college he will no longer be part of your life. That is so?'

'Friends aren't usually discarded so easily,' Alisa muttered wildly. 'I—I see him every day. He's always in and out of my room.' To her alarm the hand on hers tightened considerably, and she hastily added, 'Everybody is. I have a lot of friends we—we live very closely together. You must have been to university yourself. You know how it is.'

It was madness, standing here, shivering with cold, telling this arrogant man all about herself, explaining her actions, but she felt that she must. There was something so compelling about him that at that moment she felt as if he owned her.

He looked at her for a long time and she almost held her breath. If he didn't believe her she was quite ready to imagine that he would punish her severely. He almost seemed to have the right. She couldn't bring herself to break away from him and her eyes continually strayed to the broad expanse of his chest. She had an enormous desire to reach out and touch him, to run her hand over his strong muscles and feel the warmth of his skin.

'It's the mountains,' she suddenly blurted out, following her own chain of thought. 'It's the mountains and the moon and—and this odd place.'

'Is it?' Luc murmured. He let her hand fall, but as she was beginning to get her breath again, seeking the courage to turn away from him, he reached for her, clasping her by the waist, and before she could comprehend his intentions his mouth was covering hers with warm and insistent strength.

The gasp she uttered was forced back into her throat and he pulled her closer, his hands holding her securely, his lean fingers spread out over her spine, arching her against him. His lips were firm and cool, searching her mouth sensuously until every bit of breath left her body and she felt her legs begin to give way beneath her.

Her frantic hands that had been pushing desperately against his chest suddenly lost their will to fight and her palms flattened out against the warmth of his skin, her fingers delicately curling in the dark hair that felt crisp and clean beneath her touch.

He murmured in satisfaction at this signal of her submission and drew her further into his arms. His hand moved to cradle her head, his fingers resting beneath her hair, warmly caressing her nape, and everything inside her melted with pleasure. Without her even knowing it, her hands moved to circle his neck as her lips clung to his.

When he lifted his head Alisa just stared up at him in bewildered anxiety, and his fingers trailed down her cheek and then collected one of her hands and brought it back to his chest.

'You would have been enchanting to hold in that silky dress,' he surmised softly, his dark eyes searching her face. 'I would have felt your body closer to me.'

'How—how—?' Alisa began shakily, and he tilted her flushed face with one imperious hand, his eyes amused as he glanced at her trembling lips.

'How dare I?' he murmured. 'It was no effort, *señorita*. It required no daring, merely the inclination to reach for you. The inclination has been there for some time.' He took her hand from his chest and lifted it to his lips. '*Buenas noches*. Get some sleep. Tomorrow we arrive at the lake.'

He just walked off to his tent and Alisa almost fell into hers, her hands trembling and her legs nearly too weak to get her there. She couldn't believe it. Not only had she never even thought that he would kiss her, hold her, but she had battled with him from day one—and she knew that she should be battling with him right now. He had hypnotised her, subdued her, made her weak and feminine—and he didn't even like women!

Why had he done that? The only reason she could think of was that he had wanted to make sure that she did not venture from her tent again at night. Had he really thought she was on her way to Douglas? Somehow the thought of that made her more shaky and uneasy than anything else. The idea that Luc could imagine she would be that sort of person was horrifying.

She pulled herself together. What was she thinking? That arrogant brute had kissed her and held her tightly. Even now she could feel the way he had brought her into intimate contact with the hard warmth of his body. She shuddered, and she was honest enough to admit that it was not with revulsion. For a few minutes the whole world had drifted away—the mountains no more, the moonlight gone.

Luc had pulled her into a world she didn't recognise, a world she had never even thought of, and she curled up in her sleeping bag, her body still disturbed and trembling. She had been eager for more and she knew it. He had encouraged her to touch him and she had wanted to. If Luc had not stopped she would still have been there, locked in his arms, getting more and more involved with the moment.

Tomorrow she would have to put on a brave face, because she knew that he would simply ignore her. He would consider his actions just now either as a form of quiet discipline or an interesting experiment.

Alisa's face flushed in the darkness. She had not felt like that at all. She had been utterly submissive, completely under his spell. How she would face him tomorrow she did not know, and what her uncle would say if he knew she shuddered to think. He placed great reliance on her good sense, and it seemed that she had no sense at all.

CHAPTER SIX

DURING the middle of the morning of the next day, Alisa knew that they were very close to the mountain lake that Luc was waiting to see. Before they had broken camp and moved off her uncle had told her more or less when they expected to be there, and she knew that it would be soon.

As she had suspected, Luc had ignored her. Apart from one brief, flashing glance he had acted as if the events of the previous night had never taken place, and Alisa was bemused to find that she felt bewilderingly shy, not a state of mind she was at all used to.

She had kept out of his way, not even meeting his dark eyes when he had given her his usual swift glance of inspection. He had had no complaints; she'd had her hat on and was ready for the day.

They were travelling along a narrow trail that skirted the face of the mountains now. It was wide enough, but strewn with rocks of various sizes—not a path for the faint-hearted. This did not worry Alisa too much because she was not afraid of heights. The swaying bridge had frightened her, but here all she had to do was walk steadily on and watch her footing.

To her left, the mountain fell away into a great canyon hundreds of feet below, and there was a surprising amount of greenery clinging to the sides. This was due to the trickle of water that constantly oozed from the heights above, crossing the narrow rocky path and falling to the canyon floor. It was spectacular, but she did not feel inclined to lean over to look more closely. Every time there was a bend in the track the scene became all too obvious, and Alisa managed to keep quite calm and wait for the end of the trek.

'Not far now, Alisa,' Jeff Lane promised. He had been behind her since they had started, keeping his appointed place as Luc had first ordained it, and she had become quite used to chatting to him as they walked.

'We'll be there early,' she reminded him. 'Do you think we'll start looking today, while it's still light?'

'Maybe. At the very least, the professor and Luc will want us to search for the remains of that road we saw from the air. Once we find that I would think we'll move camp to be near it and start from there.'

'I hope I'll be useful,' Alisa muttered, and he gave a laugh at her melancholy tone.

'You can look, and that's all any of us can do—even the professor can only search.'

'Except that he'll know what he's searching for.'

'You'll know when you see it,' Jeff promised. 'It's not going to be something you'll readily overlook.'

And that was all he said, because she heard a flurry of sound and then a yell of fright and when she looked round Jeff had disappeared.

'Jeff!' Alisa screamed his name and Douglas turned, seeing what had happened and moving back towards her. By then she was lying flat, peering over the edge of the drop, her heart leaping into her throat when she saw that Jeff had managed to cling to the tough-looking bushes very near the top. Below him was the canyon and certain death, and Alisa flung her arm out with no thought of her own safety.

'Hold on! I've got you, I've got you!' she encouraged, reaching out to him as Douglas came down beside her and reached out too. But before she could get her hand to Jeff's arm she was lifted bodily out of the way and Luc took her place.

'You will stay by the wall,' he ordered. 'Move back!'

With no pause he was lying beside Douglas, his strong brown arms reaching over the sheer drop, and Alisa was terrified. Now she could appreciate that there was nothing to hold on to up here. Luc seemed to be in as much danger as Jeff, because it would have to be pure physical strength that rescued him. They could not wait for any assistance, either by ropes or with the aid of the mule. At any moment Jeff might lose his hold, or the scanty vegetation simply tear away and let him fall.

'Take my wrists,' Luc ordered, calling down. 'Try to get a grip on the rocks with your feet, or we may both be travelling downwards.'

That only served to drive home to Alisa that her thoughts had been quite true, and she could not look away even though she wanted to. She saw Luc's muscles bunch as he took most of the weight and her teeth sank into her lower lip as she watched.

He moved slowly back, and she just didn't know how he was doing it but inch by inch Jeff came up, and as his shoulders came over the top Douglas grabbed him and helped to haul him to safety. By that time Alisa was shaking like a leaf, her face white with terror.

The two men lay for a moment on the path, their eyes closed. It was too narrow for anyone else to come back and join them, but Alisa made a move to help. The dark eyes flashed open and Luc's voice stopped her in her tracks.

'You will stay there!' It was a harsh command and Alisa stopped at once, her expression woebegone. She had instinctively moved to help, to see to Jeff, but more than that she had a tremendous desire to hurry to Luc, and it was no use denying it. His eyes held her and his face softened for a second. *'Está bien,'* he assured her quietly. 'Stay by the wall.'

Alisa nodded, biting at her lip again and moving back to the hard rock of the mountain wall. She wanted to sit down but there just wasn't room. The whole expedition had come to a halt. The professor was calling to make sure everything was all right and Alisa shouted back.

By some miracle it *was* all right, a near-tragedy had been avoided and now they had to get Jeff off this abominable track. He couldn't walk without assistance. He was shaking too much and his face was a peculiar grey colour. He looked very badly battered. His clothes were torn and his head had banged against the rock. Mostly it was shock, as Alisa knew, but he could also have a broken bone or two. It had been no gentle fall and she wanted to see him as quickly as possible.

Luc and Douglas managed him between them, and as they rounded the next bend the land levelled out and there before them was the lake, ringed by the mountains, glittering in the sunlight, and quite the most welcome sight that Alisa had seen in her life. It represented safety at this moment and already her uncle and Chano were taking action, setting a fire and collecting water.

It was completely automatic for Alisa to take charge, and as soon as Jeff had been deposited on one of the groundsheets she went to him and began to feel carefully for any broken bones.

'I'm all right,' he managed in a shaken voice, and Alisa gave him a firm look.

'You're anything but all right,' she told him briskly, 'so let's not have any macho nonsense. You don't seem to have anything broken but you're bruised and battered, and the shock alone is enough to be going on with.'

She looked up and called to Chano for her bag, and while he was fetching it she began to get Jeff carefully out of his shirt. It was torn and bloodstained so she knew quite well that beneath it he would have broken skin.

There were gashes and grazes all over him. By this time almost everyone had gathered at the camp, all of them very shaken by the accident, but after checking to see that Jeff was reasonably all right they began their camp jobs and left Alisa to get on with her own task. She dressed the wounds in silence, being very gentle, because in spite of his desire to shrug the whole thing off Jeff winced frequently and he looked sick and ill.

He gave a loud yelp of surprise, however, when her hands went to the zip of his khaki trousers and she began to propel it downwards.

'That's all! I'm OK!'

'You are not OK,' Alisa insisted sharply. 'You're bleeding and probably very cut and bruised on your legs. Now, you can have these trousers off in the normal manner or I'll cut them off. Either way, you'll let me see to those other cuts and bruises. If I leave them you're very likely to get an infection.'

'Luc!' Jeff begged for support, looking up to where Luc stood watching events.

'Why protest to me?' Luc asked wryly. 'You've already had your orders from the doctor. If she can't do her job then there is not much point in her being here.' He suddenly grinned. 'You'll feel better later.'

'It's damned embarrassing!' Jeff insisted, and Alisa snorted with impatience.

'Rubbish!' she exclaimed. 'I've seen more naked men than you've had hot dinners. Douglas,' she called, 'come and assist with this touchy patient!'

It was the end of any nonsense and later, as Alisa washed her hands and rolled her sleeves down, she was confident that Jeff would be fine. He was now lying snugly in his sleeping bag, a little way from the fire, and his colour was almost back to normal. With a warm drink and a quiet time she was sure that he would be recovered by morning.

'He can't go anywhere today,' she told Luc as he came to stand by her with his coffee and handed her a steaming mug of coffee too. 'The cuts are bad but it's not that. He's suffering from shock.'

'I can see that,' he murmured. 'Fortunately we are at the lake, and there is nothing very strenuous to do now.' He looked down at her intently. 'You are alarmingly efficient. There was not much of the student there.'

'Well, I spent two years travelling around before I went to university.' She shrugged dismissively. 'I ended up in a hospital in Africa, generally helping out and sometimes almost taking over. There was a very overworked English doctor and he taught me a lot. It was way out in the bush, quite primitive at times. Anyway—' she sighed '—I learned to cope. It meant that I didn't go to university straight from school. I wasn't exactly green.'

'Green?' Luc looked at her in astonishment and she made a wry face. His English was so perfect that she expected him to know everything.

'Immature, callow, inexperienced,' she explained.

He nodded his understanding. 'The peculiarities of English. I assume that your remark about naked men and hot dinners is also an eccentricity of your language?'

Alisa gave a suppressed giggle and looked at him from her eye corners, meeting his look of quizzical interest.

'Oh, definitely an eccentricity,' she assured him with a wide grin. 'Swift action was necessary. I merely said it to calm him down.'

'I am greatly relieved to hear it,' Luc murmured. 'Now that you have set my mind at rest I will be able to calm down myself and I will not need any assistance,' he added, raising one dark brow at her and giving her a slightly reproachful look.

The professor and Douglas joined them, and Alisa was able to still her bubbling laughter. For once she had been reading Luc's mind, and she could imagine his outrage if he had taken her remarks literally. He was probably even outraged that she had said that at all, and even more outraged that with the help of Douglas she had reduced Jeff to his underwear. Luc was capable of being very straitlaced.

'Well, here's a pretty kettle of fish,' her uncle stated mournfully, and Alisa burst into laughter and grabbed his arm as Luc's dark eyes turned on the professor in exasperation.

'Just speak straightforward English,' she advised. 'Luc is already reeling from my mistreatment of the English language.'

'What?' Her uncle looked at both of them with a puzzled frown, and then decided to ignore everything in his usual way. 'What do we do now?' he asked Luc, and when Alisa looked up she was surprised to find Luc's eyes on her in an altogether softened manner.

'We eat a light lunch, rest, and then decide,' he told her uncle. 'I had hoped that we could search for the road today, but it will all depend upon how Jeff is. If he can be left, the four of us will make a small search a little later. It is up to our doctor to tell us whether or not he can be safely left here with the men and Chano.'

He looked at Alisa and she shrugged her shoulders.

'Probably,' she surmised. 'He's a big, tough man. It's just the shock. With some people it takes a while to come out. There's no way he can do any trekking today, though.'

'Then we leave it to you, *señorita*,' Luc said quietly. 'We will eat and then you can give us your opinion.'

Alisa nodded and left them as she went to have a look at Jeff. He was resting comfortably but he was not at all eager to get up and walk about. His pulse was steady and he seemed to be slowly relaxing after his ordeal, and Alisa sat on the ground beside him for a while, talking quietly and making her mind up about his condition. He was not as shocked as she had expected, but he was better off where he was. After a sleep he would be able to think about getting to his feet.

She ate her lunch sitting by him too, and she was just finishing it when she was startled to hear Luc calling her name with a great deal of urgency.

'Alisa! *Aquí*!'

She turned quickly, astonished that he had actually used her first name so readily. He was standing by the edge of the lake, binoculars in his hand, but he was facing her and beckoning to her insistently.

'*Aquí*! *Rápido*!' he called, and she was on her feet at once, running towards him, ignoring the way everyone else stared at them.

'What is it?' she asked breathlessly, and Luc's hand came to her shoulder as he pointed out across the glittering lake to the rising mountains that curved around the other side.

'*El cóndor*!' he said softly. 'First, find him, and then look through the binoculars.'

Alisa's heart leapt with excitement and she found him easily. She could see the great outstretched wings, the slow, wheeling flight, and as she focused the binoculars the bird seemed to leap at her, making her breath catch in her throat.

'It's so beautiful!' she whispered, her eyes glued to the sight, and Luc laughed softly.

'In flight, yes,' he agreed. 'Nothing is quite like it. Close up, though, the condor is not so beautiful—and yet, it is the very spirit of these mountains.'

'I could watch it forever,' Alisa murmured, and he lightly tightened his hand on her shoulder.

'I thought it would please you. Unfortunately he will not stay for long. It was a piece of good luck to even see him at all.' Even as he spoke the great bird circled in flight, soaring away behind the mountains, and Alisa lowered the binoculars and gave a sigh of pleasure.

'Thank you,' she said quietly, looking up at Luc. 'I wouldn't have missed that for anything. How did you know I wanted to see a condor?'

'I have seen your dreamy eyes,' Luc assured her, his dark gaze skimming her face and lingering on her smiling lips. 'Besides, you have been brave and efficient. You deserved a treat and the condor was the only treat available.'

'I don't know about brave,' Alisa mused. 'You had to take me over that bridge.'

'And most women of my acquaintance would have screamed and refused to go,' Luc assured her. 'Today you acted promptly and efficiently in a crisis. You did not faint and you did not demand attention yourself, although you had a shock too.' He gave her a sudden smile, his eyes narrowed and approving. 'You deserved the sight of the condor. You have earned it. If I had been able to make him stay all day for you, I would have done.'

He took her arm quite gently as they walked back together, and as Luc went to speak to her uncle Douglas commandeered Alisa.

'What was all that about?' he asked grumpily. 'You've suddenly got very chummy with your enemy.'

'It was a condor!' Alisa told him excitedly. 'Luc seemed to know that I wanted to see one. It's a thing you don't often see now. It was wonderful to watch.'

'Very good,' Douglas muttered. 'Life's full of surprises. "Alisa". "Luc". All very nice and civilised. Not two minutes ago, it seems, we had "*señorita*" on his part and "that man" on your part. Now he's getting you coffee and giving you special treats. Next you'll be holding hands!'

'Well, we did on the bridge!' Alisa snapped. 'What's the matter with you? Haven't we had enough upset for one day?'

'More than enough!' Douglas grunted, walking off, and Alisa stared after him in annoyance. What had got into him? Surely he was not jealous. He was her friend and nothing more, and even if he had been jealous, there was nothing to be jealous about. All Luc had done was show her the condor. She suddenly thought of the fact that he had also kissed her, but luckily nobody knew about that, and it was not something that would be repeated.

The memory of it disturbed her and she quickly hurried over to Jeff, her face rather flushed. She was getting too interested in Luc Sanchez and that was very silly, because when they got back to civilisation she would never see him again. That was not a very pleasing thought either, and she resolutely closed her mind to both Luc and Douglas. She had better keep thinking about the condor.

She hoped that Luc had not been remembering last night when he had said that he had seen her dreamy eyes. He had praised her bravery, and although she couldn't see at all that she had been brave it gave her a glow and made her feel worthy on this all-male trip. The women of his acquaintance would have screamed, he had said.

That brought her up sharply. According to her uncle, the women Luc knew were beautiful and passionate, quite probably the sort of females he wanted. She was treading deep water and she had better stick to her old attitude—although there was no way now that she could face Luc with the old animosity.

It was early afternoon when, after consulting her, Luc decided that a first trip could be made to try and find the road. Jeff looked much better and Alisa was happy to leave him with the Indians.

'What about Chano?' the professor asked before they set off.

'It would be better if Chano stayed in the camp,' Luc told him. 'I trust these men, otherwise I would not have brought them. They will neither steal nor abandon us. Keeping their tongues still is another matter, however. They do not know exactly why we are here and it is best if they remain in ignorance. Should we be lucky and find anything then we will need to keep it secret for a time, or others will be stamping around and ruining the site.'

'Would Chano talk?' Douglas asked, and Luc shrugged indifferently.

'Possibly not, but it is best not to single him out. Besides, he speaks English. If Jeff needs anything while we are away, Chano will understand.'

'I'll have a word with him,' Alisa decided.

By now the Indians understood that she was the doctor, and she was getting an altogether different form of respect. Their looks of admiration at her fair skin and glowing hair had now been tempered by a slight anxiety. She was important, a clever and necessary part of this expedition. She was not now merely a woman.

The new attitude was helpful in that it got things done without recourse to Luc's authority, and she had no hesitation in tackling Chano herself. He listened attentively as she told him about Jeff's shocked condition and assured him that she would not be long, and he was obviously proud to take charge.

His willing attitude reminded her about the warm water that he delivered daily, and she decided to thank him while they were speaking privately.

'Thank you for the warm water,' she said with a smile, and he looked at her as if he didn't understand at all.

'You need water, *señorita*?' he asked with a puzzled frown.

'No. I'm just thanking you for the water you put in my tent each morning,' Alisa explained. 'It's very good to be able to wash with warm water.'

'But I do not bring water, *señorita*.' Chano suddenly fathomed it out and smiled widely. 'It is the *señor*. Many times I have travelled with Señor Sanchez and he is always the first in the morning. He can rise before the sun. I have seen him bring water to your tent each day. The thanks should be for him.'

Alisa looked at him in stunned surprise, but it was clear that he was telling the truth even though it was hard to believe. Luc had seen to it that she had warm water in the mornings right from the first, even when they had been at each other's throats.

She nodded to Chano and went back to the others, somewhat subdued. It was the biggest surprise of her life that Luc should be so gallant and she went out of her way to avoid his eyes, feeling shy and rather ungrateful, even though he had no idea what she had been talking to Chano about. Thanking him at this late stage would be a bit tricky.

They set off almost at once, and in about twenty minutes the westward-bending track split in two ways.

'This was not obvious from the air,' Luc muttered, consulting the map with the professor. 'To save time it would be better to tackle both possibilities at once. I suggest that we split up—two one way and two the other.'

'Alisa can go with me,' Douglas said quickly, but before Luc could speak, the professor intervened.

'Not a good idea,' he pointed out. 'You're both new at this. One of you must go with Luc and one with me.'

It was a dilemma that Alisa was not about to get herself involved in at all. She had to admit that she wanted to go with Luc. In the first place the idea of being with him was now exciting, and also she might get the chance to mention his kindness in bringing the water. Nothing, however, would have made her make the choice herself.

'She will go with me,' Luc stated firmly, ignoring the scowl that came instantly to Douglas's face. He did not bother to explain his choice either, and simply stood with her uncle discussing the two routes.

'Very cosy,' Douglas grumbled in a low voice. 'The obvious thing would have been for you to go with the prof. He's your uncle. The only reason you're here is to look after him.'

Alisa opened her mouth to tell him sharply about his attitude, but the other two were waiting and she just went towards Luc after he had flashed a very comprehensive look at both Douglas and herself. It was embarrassing, and she knew that sooner or later she was going to have to put Douglas strictly in his place. She had never had to cope with this sort of thing before.

'It must be the mountains,' Luc murmured wryly as they moved off, 'and this odd place.'

He didn't look at her but Alisa was well able to recognise her own words of the night before, and her face flooded with rosy colour.

'Douglas is not usually a nuisance,' she muttered, avoiding looking at him.

'No doubt he will be quite normal when you are both back in England.'

She could tell by the cool sound of his voice that he had not believed her when she had explained about Douglas being a friend. Maybe in his country women did not have male friends at all. Maybe there was too much of a male-dominated attitude. She felt deflated. He was back to his normal cold attitude, and the incident with the condor might well have never happened.

After a while, with neither of them speaking, Alisa began to wish that she had insisted on going with her uncle. It didn't look as if they had chosen the right way in any case, because there was no sign of a road. Away from the lake it was barren and rocky, not a place she would have wanted to be if she was alone.

There were clumps of tufted grasses that nestled by the bigger rocks, but apart from that there was nothing to break the monotony of the barren scenery—until she looked up. The peaks still soared above them, and though she felt that they had been climbing since they had started out days ago, she knew that they had not gone very high at all. It was just the difficulty of the terrain.

'Why are you so sure that there's something to find?' she asked, when the silence stretched on endlessly.

'I am not,' Luc admitted, his eyes scanning ahead. 'I merely suspect that there is something. My ideas are simply the result of instinct and the sifting of rather wild rumours that have been circulating for a long time. Perhaps the whole trip has been for nothing.'

'All the same,' Alisa confessed, 'I wouldn't have liked to miss it. I'll never forget this trip. It's taught me a lesson too. In future I'll not worry about Uncle Bill. You were quite right. He's much more capable than I.'

'It is experience,' Luc said shortly, and Alisa glanced across at the rather tight sound of his voice.

'Jeff is experienced but he almost died back there,' she pointed out. 'It's something I'll have to face but at least I'll understand. When I knew my uncle was coming to Bolivia I was really worried. It seemed to me to be a remote and dangerous place.'

'And you have changed your mind?' Luc asked stiffly. 'I would say that you are once again judging hastily. In many ways Bolivia is a crazy place, ranging from jungle to these cold, barren heights. I can imagine that it would not appeal to an English girl.'

'It doesn't!' Alisa snapped, stung by his cold attitude. 'It's all right for a quick trip in and out. I prefer England.'

In fact she was quite able to settle anywhere. She had not had any difficulty in settling in Africa while she was working there, but Luc was annoyingly remote and cool, and the desire to strike back was never far from her. She did not have a tranquil character.

She went along silently, scowling at the ground, too annoyed even to glance at the mountains, and suddenly she saw something glitter in the rocks at the side of the track.

'Stay close!' Luc ordered as she darted off, but she ignored him. In the first place he annoyed her and in the second place she wanted to see what it was. He strode over to her angrily when she disregarded his commands, but by that time Alisa was busily scrabbling in the small rocks, her face intent as the golden object was uncovered. It was coated with dirt, almost green in places, but she had no doubt at all that it was either solid gold or gold-painted.

She pulled it out as Luc reached her and his angry words were silenced as she held it up.

'Look,' she said breathlessly. 'It's a carving of some sort. It's quite heavy.'

He didn't attempt to take it from her hand. He squatted down beside her and watched as she rubbed it on her shirt and flicked at the dirt with her thumbnail. It was glowing in the sunlight within seconds, and Alisa looked at it with excitement racing through her.

'It—it's a lion,' she muttered in astonishment. 'It's a nasty kind of lion.' It was small, small enough to hold in the palm of her hand, and it seemed to be a particularly evil lion—squatting on its haunches, its front paws on its knees. The tail was curled almost into a handle and the head was fierce, with ferocious-looking teeth.

'It is a cat,' Luc corrected softly as she placed it in his hand. 'It is the Cat God from pre-Inca times. It is solid gold. If this is here—'

'Then there may be others,' Alisa finished in excitement. 'The road might be here. It might be very close!'

They both stood and Luc looked down into her shining eyes, his mouth softening into a smile.

'How it got here I do not know. Perhaps it was dropped and forgotten, who can tell? I think, though, that the road must be close to us, as you say.'

'It's so *exciting*!' Alisa's face lit up as she looked into his dark eyes. 'Are we going back to tell the others?'

'You wish to do that?'

'No. Let's look some more! It would be wonderful if you and I found the road. My uncle would be stunned and it would make Douglas furious.'

'And you want him to be furious?' Luc asked quietly, and Alisa laughed up at him, her eyes sparkling.

'It would pay him back for being so sulky. He has no right to ask me questions and tell me what to do.'

'I must remember that,' Luc mused wryly. 'If questioned you like to pay back.'

'Oh, it's different with you,' Alisa told him ingenuously. 'You're—you're different. I couldn't have managed without you.'

'Gracias,' Luc said softly. He gave the small carving back to her. 'Put this in your pocket. You found it and it is your right to present it when we get back.'

'Is it a god that could bring me bad luck?' Alisa asked, only half joking.

'Not when I am here, *señorita*,' Luc assured her quietly. He reached for her hand and turned her back to the path. 'Come. We have about thirty minutes and then we must go back. Let us find the road and confound them all. This is something you will always remember when you are back in your safe and comfortable England.'

'I'll remember you.' Alisa said it without thinking and he swung her towards him by the hand, his dark eyes searching her face. For a second he watched her intently, and then he gave a sardonic smile and let her go.

'It would not be a good idea to remember me too well,' he advised. 'When we met you disliked me intensely. You have good instincts. I am not at all like you. For now, you are confined to a small circle of people and you need me. Do not let it colour your judgement.'

'I'm sensible,' Alisa said, quite shocked that she had spoken to him so openly. She was behaving like an idiot. 'I'm a doctor.'

'Not yet,' Luc reminded her. 'Remember your assessment of last night's events. It is the mountains and this odd place. You were quite right.'

That put her in her place very nicely and Alisa felt her cheeks glow with embarrassment. She would have been a lot more sensible if she had used the time to thank him for the warm water instead of saying that she would remember him. All the same, she *would* remember him. She had never met anyone like Luc before, and her initial antagonism had now changed to a sort of wondering awe.

Like the small creature in her pocket, Luc was a god—dark, handsome and mysterious. There was something compelling about him that drew her towards him and he was only right to warn her. In all probability he had this effect on every woman he knew.

CHAPTER SEVEN

THEY went on, climbing small rocky outcrops, doggedly following the line of the old track, and Alisa began to get very tired. Before long she was simply going forward and not even looking at all. She was almost too exhausted to lift her head when Luc suddenly took her arm and stopped her.

'Look,' he said quietly, and there in front of them was the road. It was wide, as Luc had said, paved and edged with stone. There was not much of it, but looking onward it was possible to see that it continued in sections and would look continuous from the air. This was the place that they had been looking for—the Inca road.

'We found it!' Alisa raised tired eyes to Luc, her face showing a sort of elated weariness, and his hand came out and trailed down her cheek.

'Yes, we found it,' he repeated quietly. 'Now you may punish your boyfriend and gather the glory.'

'Douglas is not my boyfriend,' Alisa muttered, dropping her head. 'You don't listen much, do you?'

'I hear what I wish to hear, see what I wish to see,' Luc informed her, and Alisa sighed tiredly.

'Then you'll always be slightly cut off from the truth,' she pointed out in an exhausted voice. 'I suppose it all comes from arrogance, but I'm too tired to argue right now.'

'No doubt you will argue later,' Luc surmised in amusement. 'We will go back now, but first you must rest. I should never have let you come so far.'

'You couldn't get rid of me,' Alisa sniffed, and he looked down at her in his old imperious manner.

'I could have let you go with the professor.'

'So why didn't you?' Alisa asked crossly, not really expecting an answer.

'Because quite obviously I enjoy your company, you foolish girl. I wanted you with me,' Luc stated flatly, and it shocked her momentarily out of tiredness. But she never got the chance to reply, because he sat down and indicated that she should do likewise. He then took a bottle of water from his small backpack and handed it to her.

'Why did you want me with you?' Alisa asked tremulously.

'I like to live dangerously. Drink,' he ordered. 'I also have some chocolate for you. It will boost your energy and save me the trouble of carrying you back to the lake.'

'You're strange,' Alisa remarked unguardedly, watching him with puzzled eyes, and he smiled his usual sardonic smile, his brown hands neatly dividing the chocolate.

'You expected that I would not be strange?' he enquired wryly. 'Perhaps, English *señorita*, you are strange and interesting to me. Perhaps that is why I kissed you last night. I have an enquiring mind.'

'And an overwhelming arrogance,' Alisa informed him sharply, coming out of her dreamy state. 'I don't take kindly to being the subject of an experiment.'

'Then do not encourage the interested party by being what you are,' he murmured silkily, watching her with dark, unfathomable eyes.

'What do you mean by that?' Alisa snapped, glaring across at him.

'You are beautiful, full of spirit and more than a little vulnerable. You invite my attention.'

'I never asked you to bring me warm water to wash with every morning!' Alisa blurted out, her cheeks hot and flustered, and a slow smile grew across his face.

'And you never told me to stop,' he pointed out.

'I thought it was Chano. I only discovered it wasn't when I asked him today. Before that I thought it was my uncle and then Douglas. I—I never thought about it being you.'

'Naturally. I am too uncivilised,' he concluded ironically, and Alisa looked at him with some exasperation.

'I thought you were too aloof, too grand, too *domineering*!' she finished heatedly. He seemed to have no difficulty in winding her up and observing her reactions with detached interest.

'But of course. I am all of those things. I am descended directly from the *conquistadores*.'

'And I'm descended from William the Conqueror!' Alisa snapped untruthfully, flinging herself back on the ground and closing her eyes, her mind seething with irritation. 'You can observe the blue eyes and fair hair!'

'I have observed,' he informed her silkily. 'It is strange. I understood that the Norman conqueror was dark.'

Alisa turned her head and shot him a look of fury, but he was also lying back, staring up at the sky, a wide grin stretched across his face, and she snorted angrily.

'*You* spoil everything!' she hissed, but all she got was a low chuckle of amusement, and she concluded that he had been entertaining himself at her expense, having nothing better to do at the moment. 'You enjoy spoiling things,' she continued angrily. 'You think you're so much more important than anyone else! You look down at people in your superior manner and—!'

Alisa gave a small cry of fear as Luc rolled over and trapped her in iron-strong arms, his body half over hers. One moment he had been looking up at the sky, laughing at her, and the next he was above her, in complete control.

'Do I?' he enquired softly. 'My superior manner has not so far deterred you from fighting me at every opportunity.' He was looking down at her with taunting eyes and Alisa felt a tingle race across her skin like a live current. She knew without being told that if she softened at all he would kiss her.

She stared up into his face and his dark eyes captured her gaze immediately, holding her fast without effort. She found her fingers curling against his shirt, her lips trembling. She wanted him to kiss her; it was obvious in her eyes. There was an air of waiting about both of them, a sexual tension singing in the air between them, and with a low mutter of impatience Luc's mouth came down on hers, his hands cupping her face as he lifted her head to his.

This time it was not the slow, sensuous exploration of her mouth that had happened before. Now the kiss was ruthlessly dominating, forcing her into a gasping acceptance of her own femininity. Her brief moment of resistance melted away. She could hear her own weak moan of submission and felt his instant response.

'You hate my superior manner, Alisa?' he asked thickly as he allowed her to tear her lips away and breathe. 'Why do you not fight it now?'

'I don't want to.'

She looked up at him with bewildered eyes and his face darkened as he bent his head again and crushed her against him, kissing her with fierce pleasure. She could feel her body softening, her arms sliding around his neck, and as Luc felt it too his hands moved over her possessively, his long fingers gently teasing her breasts.

Alisa's body leapt in shocked pleasure, melting closer to him, and for a minute he accepted this glad submission. His hands moved beneath her, moulding her dangerously close, and then he rolled away from her and stood in one lithe movement, pulling her to her feet.

'You are a dangerous temptation,' he said harshly, his hands gripping her shoulders, steadying her as she swayed. 'It will be a very good thing when we are out of these mountains and you are winging your way back to England.'

'I agree,' Alisa managed shakily. 'I don't have to defend myself against ruthless attack in England.'

'You did not defend yourself here,' Luc reminded her shortly. 'I defended you.'

'*You* attacked me!' she pointed out heatedly, angry with her own submission now that she had room to breathe and time to think.

'Is that what it was?' Luc asked lazily. 'I imagined that I was merely kissing you. I also imagined that you were enjoying the experience and begging for more. That I am apparently mistaken only serves to show the wide difference in our cultures.' He gave her a sceptical glance and then bent to collect his pack. 'Let us get back. They will be wondering where we are and your boyfriend will be quivering with suspicion.'

Alisa set her lips tightly together, not bothering to remind him again that Douglas was not her boyfriend. He knew that perfectly well and his goading was just another manifestation of his masculine arrogance.

'I hate you!' she muttered, and he didn't even bother to look at her.

'*Muy bien*!' he said coolly. 'It is better that way—much safer.'

By the time they returned to the lake her uncle and Douglas were back, both of them tired and dispirited. Jeff had managed to get up and they were all sitting around the fire. It made it easy to tell them the latest news in private and discuss the next day's action.

'Keeping this quiet will take some doing,' the professor told Luc. 'The Indians already know that we're excited about something.'

'As far as they are concerned, we have found the road,' Luc decided. 'They do not know about the golden Cat God. We will keep our camp here and leave them in it as we explore the area around the road. If it is worth further excavation then we will need to be better equipped and we will need time on our side. For this preliminary expedition they need to know nothing more.'

'You'd better keep this,' Alisa said, handing him the small creature that she had carried back to the camp, and he took it, stowing it away in his pack.

'Perhaps it would be as well if I did,' he agreed. 'We cannot simply dig things up and take them out of the country—otherwise you could keep it.'

'I wouldn't want to keep it. It would worry me,' Alisa assured him tightly. 'It may be small but it feels powerful, and I can do without uneasy thoughts of Inca retribution.'

'These mountains are getting to you,' her uncle muttered with an odd glance at her. 'I would never have believed that I would hear you speak like that.'

'Neither would I,' Alisa said shortly. 'In future, I'll leave you to your adventures and get on with my more mundane life.'

Luc slanted her an intense, dark look but she ignored it. She had finished sparring with him. She always lost and some of the things he said made her feel peculiar inside. There was heightened feeling stirring between them that was impossible to ignore. When they battled now it was almost a sexual encounter. They were even looking at each other differently, and she was smarting with humiliation at the easy way he had of subduing her.

Over the next two days, every moment was given up to the search. As yet there was nothing to excavate, and there was so little to see that had it not been for the Cat God it would have been easy to think that there was nothing but the road. All the same, there must have been a reason for this road, and nothing could obliterate the fact that the golden image was now secure in Luc's possession.

It was Douglas who finally made the discovery. They had all been working hard. Jeff was now recovered and the five of them were just about to give up for the day when Douglas found a small opening almost hidden behind a fall of rock. It was sufficiently interesting to have them spend the time removing the debris that had lain there for so many years, and when the gap was wide enough for squeezing through they found exactly what Luc and the professor had been searching for.

Beyond the narrow gap was an open area like a small arena, and without any digging at all it was obvious that a building had been here. The foundations were still intact, in some places at least four feet high, and the plan of the building was all that the professor needed to see.

'A small replica of a temple,' he said quietly. 'Probably all they had time to construct.' He stood and regarded it sombrely. 'You see, the Spaniards were coming—the *conquistadores*. They would have saved what they could, hidden in the mountains, and a temple, however miniaturised, would have been the only fitting place for the remaining treasures.'

'Why didn't the Spaniards search?' Douglas asked solemnly, catching some of the professor's mood.

'There was silver—a mountain of it. And there was gold for the taking—precious stones and riches beyond their imagination,' Luc reminded him quietly. 'Why should they pursue a few relics? It would not have been worth the effort even if they had known of this place—which they probably did not.'

They were all silent. Whatever they eventually found here did not seem to matter at this moment. There was an atmosphere of mystery, of dedication, and a lingering melancholy. The sun blazed into the small amphitheatre and Alisa could almost feel the despair of a conquered race.

'We need a lot of time and we need help,' Alisa's uncle stated, coming out of his gloomy contemplation of the scene. 'It's pointless to touch this place now. This is a big project.'

'Then we may as well return to La Paz,' Luc suggested. 'We can discuss this in more comfortable surroundings and plan our return.'

For now, the excitement was over. There was the return trip and after that, for Alisa, nothing. Before the main expedition was mounted she would be back in England, taking up the rest of her training at the hospital. Now that it was over she felt a great sense of loss. For a while she had lived a different life, been in a different world, and had met a man like Luc Sanchez. Now she would be back to normal. It was more than a let-down but there was nothing she could do about it.

Luc gave her an intense, sidelong glance as they walked back, and for a second she met his dark eyes.

'The find has depressed you,' he surmised, and Alisa looked away, shrugging her shoulders.

'A little. Your ancestors have a lot to answer for, Señor Sanchez.'

'Perhaps,' he agreed with an amused look at her tight expression. 'But I can guarantee that you would not have been at all enchanted to meet an Inca warrior, Señorita Fenton. You are even afraid of the relic you found. Chano and his friends are impressed by your fair beauty. Their ancestors would probably have been more impressed. They would have sacrificed you to the moon and expected great rewards to follow.'

'Well, I'll not be coming again,' Alisa said huffily. 'When the expedition makes its way here next time, I'll be working all hours in some hospital.'

'It is well,' Luc told her shortly. 'I would not allow you to come a second time.'

'You mean I've been a nuisance!' Alisa stated angrily, turning on him. They were well behind the others now, and she could show her annoyance without upsetting her uncle.

'You have not been a nuisance,' Luc assured her quietly, looking down at her. 'But I would not again risk your life. Neither would I allow you to face hardships.'

'I'm tough,' Alisa said with a slight look of anxiety at his intent expression.

'You are a woman,' Luc said darkly. 'That brings its own problems. You worry about your uncle. I can tell you most categorically that he worries about you also.'

'But he hasn't worried while I've been here,' Alisa protested, and Luc gave her a wry look that silenced her.

'I assured him from the first that I would take care of you,' he said. 'It left him with an easy mind.'

'So everything was planned,' Alisa said, a forlorn expression on her face. 'And your acts of kindness were just—just...'

'I am not kind, Alisa,' Luc informed her in a suddenly harsh voice. 'You did not find me kind when we first met and I can assure you that I have not changed.

All I have to do now is get you back to the hotel. I can then continue to be what I am. It will not distress you because you will be back in England, safe and comfortable.'

The conversation left Alisa feeling shattered, and although she argued with herself that she was not at all surprised by the facts she had learned, the excitement went out of everything. It brought home to her very clearly that much of the excitement had been due to the growing feelings between them, and that had all been a sham.

Alisa looked after the others as they disappeared round a bend in the track. Suddenly she was lonely.

'I wish I'd never come,' she said in a low voice, and Luc looked down at her, his face tight and strained.

'So do I,' he grated. 'I would never have seen you and that would have been better for both of us.'

'What does it matter?' Alisa asked with shaky defiance. 'I'll forget all this and you the moment I'm on the plane.'

Luc gave a growl of anger and reached out, his arms lashing round her before she could move, and Alisa gasped with shock as he brought her into contact with his strong body. Before she could struggle his lips covered hers impatiently, his kiss filled with a hungry intent that was unmistakable.

She pulled her head way, fighting the urge to sink into his masculine power, and he looked down at her frantic face with blazing eyes, his arms refusing to release her.

'Has my uncle asked you to kiss me too?' she managed with trembling anger, and he gave a low grunt of annoyance, his hands tightening almost to the point of pain.

'No, he has not. Neither has he asked me to desire you. Some things I do for myself, and wanting you is one of them. If we were alone, I would take you now and you would not resist at all.'

His head swooped down to hers again, and this time Alisa offered no resistance. When his lips searched hers with the same hungry anger she gave in, melting against him, and after a second her arms slid round his neck, accepting what Luc had put into words. There was a fiery attraction between them and it had been there from the moment they met—from the moment his hands had touched her in the moonlit garden.

As he felt her resistance melt Luc's hands moved to cup her face, holding it up to his, his mouth draining hers until she was trembling and weak. It was almost a shock when he lifted his head and firmly put her away from him.

'Come along,' he ordered huskily. 'We must join the others.'

When she just stood there, shaking and bewildered, he turned back to her and his hand closed around her wrist as he pulled her forward.

'I—I can't—' she began, but he stopped and tilted her flushed face to his.

'You can. This is madness and we both know it. When you are back in La Paz you will forget this, and if you remember it will be with a good deal of annoyance.' He looked down at her quizzically, his own composure completely restored. 'I do not imagine that you normally allow a man to hold you and kiss you as the mood takes him. I do not suppose that you offer no resistance when he also threatens to possess you. Here, we are in another world, out of time. It is easy to act unusually.'

Alisa looked at him almost wildly, his words sinking into her spinning thoughts. She would not allow a man to hold her and kiss her unless she wanted to be kissed, and she knew that perfectly well. She would not nestle against him either, and long for more, and this was nothing to do with being in the mountains. It was the powerful feelings that flashed between them.

Luc stared into her eyes, his dark gaze seeing far too much, and she dropped her head, setting off with him to join the others, her hands now clenched at her sides as she tried to stop them trembling. It was purely sexual attraction, and she supposed that she would have felt it long ago with someone else if she hadn't been too busy studying and racing round guarding her uncle.

Next morning they began the trek back to civilisation, and the first thing they had to do was walk along the narrow track where Jeff had so nearly lost his life. Alisa knew that it took a good deal of courage on his part to step out again along the narrow pathway, and she was not nearly so sure of herself as she had been when they had come along on their way to the lake.

She had expected Luc to issue lectures and warnings but he said nothing, and she assumed that it would have made Jeff feel less of a man. He said very little to her either. All he said was, 'Stay close to the wall and watch where you put your feet.' It was advice she had already decided upon herself.

There was no further trouble until they came to the hanging bridge. Each night they camped where they had been before and things went on as normal, although the nightly meal was a little more frugal. They could not have stayed longer by the lake because they would have run out of food, and now that they were using up their supplies Alisa could see that it had all been planned for exactly the time they had taken.

She had been thinking about the bridge all morning, and she had decided that this time she would nonchalantly cross with the others. When she actually saw it, though, her courage deserted her, and she stopped and stared at it in fright.

'I'll take you across,' Douglas offered when he saw the expression on her face and she actually stepped forward with him, but before she had even one foot on the swaying bridge she knew that she could not. She needed Luc's strength, his unshakeable calm. Douglas was likely to joke as they went across, and it was no joke to her.

She looked up in desperation and found Luc's dark gaze upon her.

'I can't,' she whispered, and he came forward without a word, took her hand and stepped to the bridge, taking her with him.

This time he didn't attempt to hold her interest with conversation, and she felt that he was angry at having been placed in such an embarrassing position. Her lips trembled and she felt so ashamed that tears actually came into her eyes.

'I'm sorry,' she muttered. 'I never meant to ask you to take me across. I really thought I could do it myself. Douglas would have made me even more frightened.'

Luc didn't say anything and she bit at her lip, seeing the situation all out of proportion.

'Please speak to me,' she begged quietly, and Luc glanced down at her and noticed the look on her face.

'What shall I say to you? I have told you already about the bridge. I have assured you of your courage. You and I do not easily make casual conversation. Do not be afraid. You are safe with me and I will get you back to La Paz. That is all that matters.'

There was no answer to remarks like that, and Alisa blinked the tears away and tried not to think of anything but the safety of the other side.

'Alisa,' he said softly after a second, when she kept resolutely silent. 'Forget this time in Bolivia. It would have been better if you had never come, if we had never met.'

'Do you have to be so cruel?' Alisa asked in a choked voice, her emotions a turmoil inside.

'Perhaps I do. You know quite well what is simmering between us. It would be very easy to let things take their course. I enjoy having you with me and reaching for you would be the most natural thing in the world. It is what I want to do. But you do not belong here. I have been to England. I went there to university. I am Bolivian and my life is here. You will be an English doctor. We have nothing in common at all.'

'I—I never thought we had,' she managed shakily. 'You're imagining that...'

'I have never been an idiot,' Luc rasped. 'I know how you look at me. I know how I feel about you. I want you, and the sooner I get you out of these mountains and back to civilisation the better it will be. You and I have been playing a dangerous game of hide and seek since we met. If you stay near me I will catch you, and you will not like the consequences.'

They reached the other side and Luc immediately let her hand fall as he signalled for the others, and Alisa had just that time to pull herself together and try to appear normal before she had to face interested eyes. Luc did not look at her and there was nothing she could say. For once in her life she had to take what was meted out and keep silent.

It was noticeable that the others returned to fairly high spirits long before they were out of the mountains. There was another expedition to plan and Douglas was assured of a place on it. He and the professor spent a lot of time talking. They would have to arrange their times to fit in with university terms and the professor's commitments. Jeff, too, was rethinking his own schedules, and they could all see the prospect of an early return to the Andes.

Luc went back to being dark and silent and Alisa felt utterly left out. Not too long ago she had seemed to be an important member of this male-dominated party, now she was merely at the edge of things. Mostly it was because she had withdrawn mentally from everything—she could not fault Luc's logic and she knew that he had only spoken the truth.

She had been attracted to him more and more as the days had passed, and he had softened towards her during that time. Now when his eyes met hers she always looked away speedily, because she knew that if he came and drew her away from the glow of the camp-fire and took her in his arms she would not resist. The knowledge made her feel shaken and bewildered, and she was glad when finally they were on the last leg of their journey back.

They could see the Land Rovers as they came over the last rise. The vehicles were drawn up waiting for them and soon they would be driving away—all this over for Alisa. They began to descend the rocky track, and whether it was tiredness or sheer carelessness because the end was in sight Alisa did not know, but suddenly her feet failed to find a secure foundation.

She slipped on the loose rocks, and instead of careering into Douglas, who was still in front of her, Alisa slid sideways. There was nothing to stop her as she overbalanced and went hurtling down the precipitous slope towards the Land Rovers.

It was impossible to clutch at anything, and though she vaguely heard voices calling her name, she could only feel the pain as she banged into rocks and went hurtling downwards, crashing into every obstacle with no way of stopping. There was a terrible pain in her leg, and when she finally fetched up against a huge boulder her head crashed into it and blackness engulfed her instantly.

Alisa could remember nothing but pain, vague recollections of arms holding her, a hand cradling her head, and each slight memory was surrounded by black depths of oblivion. She remembered white walls, the smell of antiseptic and grave faces bending over her, but there was never a face that she knew. Each time she tried to speak or move she was restrained, the blackness racing back to cut off the pain.

When she finally came round completely she knew at once that it had been no pain-filled dream. The room was the same and Alisa turned her head carefully to find the worried blue eyes of her Uncle Bill watching her.

'You're back with us,' he said, his hand covering hers. 'How do you feel, Alisa?'

'I'm not sure. I'll let you know.' She managed a smile and then asked, 'Where am I?'

'You're in a clinic in La Paz. Getting you here was a problem, and that's an understatement. Getting you back to anywhere was a nightmare.' He leaned forward and squeezed her hand urgently. 'Alisa, my dear, if anything happened to you I would never forgive myself. I can't tell you what you mean to me.'

'Well, I'm alive,' Alisa assured him with a weak smile, tears filling her eyes at this unusual emotion from her uncle. 'I feel a bit odd, though. What happened to me?'

'A badly cut leg and a fractured skull. Mercifully it was only a hairline fracture, but it's kept you pretty much unconscious for almost a week. When you went hurtling past me and hit that huge rock I thought you would be dead, and I can tell you I was useless in the crisis. All I could do was shout your name. If it hadn't been for Luc I don't know what would have happened.'

'Luc?' Alisa asked worriedly, and for the first time she saw a slight smile light up her uncle's face.

'Surely you haven't forgotten him?' he asked with wry humour. He shook his head in bemusement. 'I've never known anyone like him. He's utterly unshakeable. He just went ploughing down amongst the rocks to you with no thought for his own safety, and before we had even joined him he had you up in his arms and was heading for the Land Rovers. When I got to him he just abandoned the others and we were off. Jeff had to organise the rest of the withdrawal. Luc didn't even speak to any of the others. All he did was grind out orders to me.'

'Luc drove me here?' Alisa asked, but the professor shook his head and looked quite proud of himself.

'I drove you here. Luc sat and held you. There was no way you could be put in the back and subjected to that rough ride. I drove and Luc held you as safely as he could. Luckily you were unconscious most of the time. I'm not the world's best driver and some of the things Luc called me were outside my understanding of Spanish—which was probably as well. Being sworn at savagely in a foreign language doesn't do much for the confidence.'

'I—I suppose he was angry,' Alisa muttered anxiously, and the professor grinned widely.

'Well, I hope so—otherwise there's no excuse for his fluent castigation of your poor old uncle.'

'He would have been angry with me for being careless,' Alisa corrected him, but her uncle looked at her in astonishment.

'Careless? Of course you were not careless. You're a very competent young lady. Nobody called Jeff careless when he fell off the mountain. These things happen. No, Luc blamed himself, me, Bolivia, the Andes—and I do believe that in the tirade he mentioned the Incas in less than glowing terms.'

It was a great relief and there was no use denying it. The thought that even at the last minute she had been a nuisance to Luc would have worried her terribly, and Alisa wondered where her boundless self-confidence had gone.

'I promise not to try and take care of you again, Uncle Bill,' she said shakily, and he smiled at her with his usual affection.

'Don't change your gentle tyranny,' he begged. 'I would miss it enormously. Dodging round you makes life one long excitement. Not that you'll get the chance for a while,' he added quietly. 'You're not fit to fly back home yet.'

'It must be costing a fortune here,' Alisa surmised worriedly. The room was luxurious. Now that she was conscious she could see that the white walls were the only sign that this was not a room in some affluent household. It was obviously a private clinic, and her uncle, for all his fame, was not a wealthy man—and she was merely a student as yet.

'This is courtesy of the Sanchez Mining Company,' Uncle Bill informed her. 'Luc came striding in here, carrying you as if you were bone china and issuing orders as he went. For all I know, the Sanchez Mining Company owns this place. Everyone came to attention as they saw him and trotted after him as he passed. Even if he doesn't own it, he was in the mood to buy the place and sack them all if they made one false move.'

'Oh, gosh!' Alisa muttered. Thinking of Luc when he was only slightly annoyed was worrying enough. 'So how long must I stay here?' she asked, and her uncle looked a little put out.

'They say a couple of weeks,' he told her. 'The trouble is, my dear, I have to get back. When they think you're safe to leave, you're going to Luc's house. His mother is coming to look after you.'

CHAPTER EIGHT

'UNCLE BILL! I can't!' Alisa gasped. 'I hardly know Luc. I don't know his mother at all. It's such a dreadful imposition.'

'Listen,' he said quietly, his hand stilling her agitated fingers. 'I nearly lost you. I'm taking no further chances. It will be some time before you can fly back home. The leg has to mend and a fractured skull is no small thing. They'll want to watch you here for at least a week, but even then you'll still be a semi-invalid. You know all this, Alisa. I don't really have to tell you.'

'It's not that,' she protested. 'How can I just force my company on Luc and his family?'

'If Luc were in England and hurt, wouldn't we take care of him?'

'Of course we would!' Alisa said indignantly, and he nodded with satisfaction.

'That's exactly what Luc pointed out to me when I protested about this. There's no moving him. He insists, and I must say I'd rather leave you with Luc than anybody in the world other than Betsy. And I also have to say that Betsy doesn't have Luc's strength—nor his caustically fluent Spanish,' he added with a rueful grin. 'Really, my dear, you'll love Luc's house.'

'You mean you've been there already?'

'Many times. I've known Luc for years—ever since he was a student in England. It's funny to think that a chance meeting should end like this. He came to one of my lectures when I was in London and afterwards he waited to speak to me. His knowledge of South American cultures impressed me so much that I arranged to meet him again. After that we got on very well. I've stayed at his house every time I've been anywhere near here. It's not far from Sorata, and that's one of the most beautiful places I've ever seen. You'll love it.'

As far as Alisa could see there was no getting out of it, and she dreaded the sight of Luc. Whatever her uncle said, and no matter how Luc insisted on showing gallant old-fashioned hospitality, she felt as if she had brought disaster to the whole expedition and a great deal of nuisance value to Luc himself.

Even without all that there was this feeling between them. Luc had said that it was a good thing she was leaving, and now, because she had fallen, because he felt responsible, he was insisting that she stayed at his own house. He would be polite and courteous but he would resent it. How could he do otherwise?

Douglas came in to see her later and he was a welcome sight. He sat by the bed and stared at her for a minute, and then started off with the old student quips.

'Of course, you did this deliberately to get first-class attention,' he joked, and Alisa tried to reply in kind. But somehow the time in Bolivia had changed her entirely. She felt much older than Douglas now, and it wasn't just the accident. She had been gradually changing without even realising it, and she knew that it was because of her awareness of Luc. She had never had any serious feelings for anyone before and she was never going to be the same again. She longed to see Luc, but dreaded it. She had never been in such a turmoil inside.

'I want to go home,' she told Douglas seriously after a while, and he looked at her uneasily.

'You can't, Al, and you know that,' he reminded her. 'I wish we could all stay with you, but apart from university and the need to rearrange things, we just can't afford to stay. It's been eating at the prof ever since you had the fall. It took Luc a whole evening to persuade him that he was fit to take care of you.'

'Luc?' Alisa asked. 'I thought you resented him?'

'I never did until I saw you getting too chummy with him,' Douglas confessed. 'It was pretty stupid of me even then. I know I'm your best pal. But being irritated with him now is just not on the cards. Without him you would be dead, in all probability, and he's taken both your uncle and me under his wing.' He suddenly grinned. 'And there was I thinking you were the only one with a mother hen complex. Mind you,' he added more seriously, 'the prof was in a bad way. Somehow I've never thought of him as your uncle before; he's just been the prof. He loves you a lot.'

'He brought me up,' Alisa said softly. 'He's the only family I have. Maybe now you understand why I worry about him?'

'He worries about you,' Douglas pointed out, and it reminded her of Luc's words when they were in the mountains. He had done everything for her uncle's peace of mind, and no doubt this hospitality was for the same reason.

She did not see Luc for two days, and during that time Alisa began to feel much better. The headaches were still bad but she was feeling stronger, and although she could not get out of bed she was able to sit up and take at least a little food. She was treated like a queen, and if it had not been so astonishing it would have been most embarrassing. When she tentatively mentioned it to the English-speaking doctor she saw every day, he reminded her that she was the only fair-haired woman in the place, and as such she was a novelty.

It was very tactful, but she knew it was Luc's authority and wealth that kept everyone on their toes to such a ridiculous extent. She saw her uncle and Douglas each day, but it did not lessen the impact when they told her that they would have to leave in two days' time.

That evening Luc came, and Alisa was completely unprepared for his visit. She had not even thought that he would come at all. He had not been so far and she had assumed that he would have her collected when the time came to leave the clinic. After all, she was nothing to him. He just expected to take care of anyone who was with him. It was no different from the way he had ordered everyone to bed at the hotel on that first night.

It had all added to her uncertainty. The thought of simply being taken to his house to face strangers, however kind, had been worrying her ever since her uncle had mentioned the plans for her convalescence. She felt very vulnerable and utterly unable to take care of herself for the first time in her life.

Evidently they had collected her luggage, because she had her own nighties with her, and she tried to make herself presentable each day. Even so, she felt all manner of a wreck when she looked up as the door opened and found Luc's eyes on her in their intent way.

He had a huge bouquet of brilliant flowers in his hand, and at least that brought a smile to Alisa's lips. Both her uncle and Douglas had brought flowers, but nothing so grand and exotic as these. Luc caught her expression and glanced round the room, seeing the other arrangements.

'You think I have overdone it, hmm?' he asked in his usual astute way, but he was smiling and it made things easier. 'How do you feel?' he continued, putting the flowers down and sitting by the bed.

'Much better, thank you. In a couple of days I expect they'll take the bandage off my leg.'

'You are very pale,' he insisted, looking at her closely. 'Paler than you were when you first came to Bolivia. The head is troubling you?'

'Not very much. I'm a little uncomfortable but that's all. I'm lucky to feel so much better, considering the fall.'

'I thought you were dead. When I reached you I could not at first find a pulse.' He looked at her seriously. 'You must take care when they allow you to get out of bed.'

'Maybe I could fly back home before long,' Alisa began, hurrying to get the words out. 'I know I can't go with my uncle and Douglas, but I could go soon. I've got my return ticket and—'

'No!' Luc stated uncompromisingly. 'It will be some time before you are fit to travel, and even then I would hesitate to send you alone on such a journey.'

'But I can't just stay,' she pleaded. 'I can't just stay at your house, as my uncle says.'

'Why not? My mother has agreed to come and stay also. I will be there for only a small amount of time. Work has piled up for me while I have been on this trip, so you would not be in any way compromised by my presence.'

'I didn't mean that!' Alisa protested. 'I'm not bothered about silly conventions. It's just that—that I'll be a guest you can't get rid of, and I'll feel uncomfortable.'

'We will not wish to get rid of you,' Luc assured her with a sudden wry glance. 'Perhaps if you stop behaving like a poor little stray cat you will see that it is necessary and sensible.'

'I'm not behaving like a stray cat,' Alisa began heatedly, and his lips twisted in amusement as he met the angry blue of her eyes.

'Storm at me,' he encouraged softly. 'At least I know you are recovering when your temper rises.' He took her hand in his and looked at her seriously. 'I have regretted speaking to you so harshly at the end of the journey, but then, I did not know you were going to be hurt. If you stay with us willingly I will know you have forgiven me. My mother is looking forward to having someone of her own race to stay. She is willing to remain in my house until you are well enough to go back to England.' He gave her a swift glance of mockery. 'Even if she leaves, you have already stated that silly convention does not worry you. There are servants in the house and I am utterly trustworthy.'

'Oh, please...' Alisa began in embarrassment, and he relented, letting her hand go and sitting back.

'You will stay at my house until you are very fit,' he ordered. 'Let us consider that arranged.'

'I have no alternative,' she sighed, and he nodded with every appearance of satisfaction.

'No, you do not. Once again, I am able to order you about.'

'Just like old times,' Alisa sniffed.

'Not exactly,' he reminded her quietly. 'Things changed. If I recall, my orders did not continue all the time.'

She felt her face beginning to flush with colour, and rushed into words to get herself out of the predicament.

'I seem to have taken up a lot of your precious time.'

'You are not too much trouble. Fitting you into my busy schedule has been no great hardship. In any case, I could not have let you fly back to England without saying goodbye properly. Now I have the time to change things.'

'I—I don't really know what you mean by that,' she murmured, and he looked at her ironically as he stood to leave.

'Of course you do not,' he agreed. 'You have already informed me that I am strange. Perhaps before you leave Bolivia you will think I am even more strange. It remains to be seen. There is plenty of time.'

Alisa sat looking at the door after he had left, trying to work all that out, but she had to give it up. It was enough for now that she had had her worries settled. She was no longer anxious about going to stay with Luc. She was glad that she would see more of him. A few more memories to make.

There would be the memory of the mountains and the mystical flight of the condor. Other than that it would all seem like a dream. Luc would be a magnificent picture in her mind to last forever. At least she would be able to look cheerful when her uncle left with Douglas. She could pretend it was a holiday. She could pretend that Luc Sanchez was just a wealthy, important person she had met during a brief visit to Bolivia.

Waiting to leave the clinic seemed endless. When her uncle left for England he was inclined to be more emotional than Alisa, and even Douglas behaved a little gruffly, patting her hand in an agitated sort of way and finally kissing her cheek.

'Watch out for Sanchez, Al,' he muttered before he left. 'I know he's a fascinating devil, but he's not like us at all. He's very...'

'Foreign?' Alisa asked wryly, and he looked a bit embarrassed.

'You know what I mean,' he stressed. 'I don't really think you're a match for him. I've seen you skittle other people, but let's face it, he reduced you to size in no time.'

'You're talking yourself into trouble,' Alisa pointed out in amusement. 'I'll not always be incapacitated. I'll be back to get you before long, and then look out.'

'Just see that you are,' Douglas warned. 'You could get hurt here, and I don't just mean in the Andes.'

'I'll be back,' Alisa promised quietly. 'Nobody is going to hurt me.'

He looked doubtful, and when he had gone Alisa wondered what had brought that brotherly lecture on. She hoped that her fascination with Luc was not obvious to anyone other than Douglas. Of course, she had known Douglas for a long time. He would have seen the change in her and she was not given to fooling herself. She had changed and it was only because of Luc. And as to hurting her, he already had—on several occasions.

When the time finally came for Luc to take her to his house she had managed to let herself get nervous again. This was because he had not been to see her in a whole week, and with her uncle and Douglas back in England she had been lonely and had had plenty of time to work herself up into a state of anxiety.

The bandage was off her leg and she had been given physiotherapy, which had helped. She was not quite steady on her feet yet, but the exercises she had been instructed to do would get her back to normal quickly. Apart from that she was well again, and though she was still pale, Alisa felt almost back to normal.

Luc came one morning to collect her, and she was already dressed and waiting for him. She had put on her cream dress again, and the realisation that she had brought only one other dress had made her start worrying about what she was going to wear while she was staying at Luc's house.

'You are anxious about something,' Luc said astutely as he settled her into his car. 'Is it because you are still not walking properly or is it because you are with me? I thought we had dispelled your fears about staying at my house?'

'It's not that,' Alisa assured him quickly. 'It's only a silly little thing.' He turned to look at her and showed no inclination to start the car until she answered.

'Tell me about this silly little thing,' he said softly. 'I will deal with it.'

'You can't deal with everything,' Alisa pointed out, but when he went on looking at her and waiting implacably she had to speak. 'It's just that I only brought two dresses,' she confessed. 'I don't know how long I'm going to be at your home, but....'

'You will buy more dresses,' Luc announced, leaning forward and starting the car. 'If you feel able, I will drive you to La Paz. If you are not well, I will have them sent for you.'

'It's not quite so simple,' Alisa protested. 'I can't rush off to buy new clothes. I'm a student. I'm poor.'

'I am not,' Luc informed her imperiously. 'You may have anything you wish.'

'You know perfectly well that I'll not allow you to buy me things,' Alisa said emphatically, her face flushed and disconcerted, and he slanted her a quizzical look.

'Why not? You think it would compromise you? *Muy bien*. I will do it stealthily.'

'You're embarrassing me,' Alisa muttered, looking down at her tightly clasped hands. 'Perhaps in your country something like buying clothes for females means nothing, but in England....'

'I do not mean to distress you,' Luc assured her quietly. 'I am a practical person and this seems to be a practical solution to your problems. Be sensible, Alisa. You did not intend to stay in Bolivia for so long and you are unprepared. There must be many things that you need. Allow me to buy them. It will ease my guilty conscience, because I have been berating myself for ever allowing you to go with us into the mountains.'

'I managed until the last minute,' Alisa reminded him desperately, and he gave a grunt of annoyance and turned his attention to the road.

'At the last minute,' he stated harshly, 'you were almost killed. It is a miracle that you survived that fall. If you had been a child in hospital I would have brought you toys. You are not a child. I will buy you some dresses and anything else you need. It is settled. I do not wish to discuss it again.'

'You're very arrogant,' Alisa stated ruefully. It was impossible to be angry with someone who insisted on treating her like this.

'I cannot help it,' Luc informed her drily. 'It is built into my character, passed down from my ancestors.'

'Then it ought to have improved with time,' Alisa murmured, and he glanced at her in amusement.

'You think so? You have not yet seen my father. If you insist that I am arrogant then you will have to invent a new word for him. When compared with my father, I am meek and retiring. Of course,' he added when she looked up at him in alarm, 'you may not see him while you are staying with me. But I warn you, *señorita*, that if he decides to visit you will be well advised to hide.'

'By then I'll probably be back at home,' Alisa said hopefully.

'We will see,' Luc said smoothly. 'My mother is delighted to be asked to stay and look after you. She will be loath to let you go.'

'Look,' Alisa managed, alarm growing by the second, 'I'm quite fit to travel to England now. I'm still limping, but flying back would be no problem.'

'It would be a problem for me,' Luc assured her. 'I would be worried, and that would be an entirely new experience for me. You have been hurt in Bolivia. I must make it up to you.'

'You're unfathomable,' Alisa murmured, utterly agitated by now. 'You owe me nothing. You can't take on the responsibility for everyone hurt in Bolivia.'

'No, I cannot,' he agreed. 'I would never attempt such a task. However, you are not just anyone. I intend to look after you.'

'Jeff was hurt,' Alisa reminded him with anxious frustration. 'Look after him.'

'He was merely grazed. You dealt with him yourself. In any case, he is not nearly as beautiful.' He suddenly laughed aloud and shook his head in amusement. 'Let it go, little firebrand. You are with me and that is an end to the matter.' Alisa looked even more alarmed and his face softened. 'I have not kidnapped you. It will not be necessary to fight your way out.'

Alisa was silent. She didn't feel that it would be necessary to fight her way out, and in any case, now that she was out of the clinic she didn't feel nearly as fit as she had done. It was just that Luc alarmed her, and hearing about his father had done nothing to set her mind at rest. If his father came and was annoying she would have to hold her tongue because she was a guest.

Now that she was back with Luc she felt the same old tingle of expectation, and this stay in his house would only make matters worse. She should have insisted upon going home, but, as he had pointed out, it was too late now. She would just have to take great care to be coolly and politely English. Nobody could object to that, and if Luc's father was as cold as ice and very formal then he would probably appreciate formal behaviour.

From La Paz they were driving into the region of the Yungas, the valleys that swept down from the *altiplano*, and the difference in climate was soon obvious. It was sub-tropical, warm, even though there were still magnificent mountain views, and as the car descended from a spectacular, high mountain pass Alisa fell silent and drank in the sight of the fertile valley spread below them.

The sun was slanting through drifting mist; she could see ancient Inca terraces, and as they dropped even lower plantations of bananas and coffee. There were small Indian villages too, and lush vegetation, and it was so very different from the landscape in the Andes that Alisa felt disorientated. It was like another country.

'Are we close now?' she asked quietly, and Luc nodded.

'Reasonably close. You will like Sorata, *señorita*. It is one of the most beautiful places in South America. It has been compared to the Garden of Eden. My house is not too far from there. It is on the slopes of the mountain that we call Illyampú. From the terraces you can see the mountains, with snow always on their heights. In the distance, you will see the town of Sorata. It is peaceful. I come back to relax and recapture my sanity. You will get well here.'

As he spoke he turned the car from the road, and they began to travel another road that had been carved into the hills. It was wide, not the sort of alarming road they had driven over from La Paz, where they had been dodging lorries and other vehicles. This road was tranquil and empty, and as they came to huge carved gates set into tall stone pillars Alisa realised why there were no other vehicles about. This was a private road.

Luc leaned out and spoke into a grille set into the high pillar at the side nearest to the driver.

'Sanchez!' he said curtly. '*Abran la puerta*!'

There was a whir of sound and the huge carved gates opened silently, closing behind them as they drove through, and Alisa had the sense of entering a stronghold. This was the domain of a very rich man, and she was sitting right beside him.

'We have arrived,' Luc told her quietly and she nodded, suddenly unable to speak.

'You are afraid?' He glanced at her quickly and noticed her expression. 'Why? Nobody will hurt you. Or is it me? Is it because I am so very different from you?' His voice hardened as he said that, and Alisa hurried to dispel that idea.

'It's just that you're very rich,' she said in almost a whisper, and he brought the car to a halt, turning to look at her. When she went on avoiding his gaze he tilted her face, his strong fingers under her chin.

'That makes me unacceptable? You would feel safer if I was a poor man?' He looked into her blue eyes and then his hand slid gently round her face. 'This is my home, Alisa,' he said softly. 'It has always been my home. My father was wealthy from birth and now the burden is mine. He lives with my mother in La Paz, his responsibilities over. I have merely taken up the reins as they fell. I knew always that it would be my duty. Beneath it all, I am just a man like any other. Do not be afraid. I will take care of you.'

His eyes moved to her soft lips and then searched her face, and she knew that he saw the expression there, her anxiety mixed with her utter fascination with him.

'Do not look at me like that,' he ordered thickly. 'You are temptation enough, and I must not forget that now you rely on me. I cannot now reach for you when the mood takes me.'

'Why?' Alisa asked guilelessly, unaware of what she was saying, and his hand tightened against her face, his head bending towards her before he suddenly pulled away and sat back, taking a deep breath.

'*Dios*!' he growled. 'Do not make me behave like a villain. You are inviting the very thing you fear. The sooner you are safely with my mother, the better it will be.'

'I—I'm sorry,' Alisa muttered, her face flushed and embarrassed. 'I don't know why I said that.'

'You said it because you feel what I feel,' he said harshly. 'I find you even more desirable now that you are so vulnerable. But I did not bring you here to make love to you. I owe you safety. When I am sure you are settled I will leave. It will be the wisest thing to do.'

Alisa agreed with everything he said, and she felt shy and ashamed. He had seen how she reacted to him and known she had wanted him to hold her. She felt safe when he held her but he was pointing out that the safety would not have lasted. She knew that perfectly well, but it didn't make a lot of difference.

'I don't want you to leave,' she admitted in a low voice, her head dropping to hide her face. 'If you're not there...'

Luc reached across and collected her, pulling her into his arms and lifting her face to meet his.

'Nothing will hurt you,' he promised huskily. 'Nobody would even think of it, and even if the idea crossed their minds, they would not dare. I am not a forgiving enemy. Already the people in my household know that I care for your safety and comfort. They will guard you.'

'I'll be lonely,' Alisa whispered, looking up at him with wide, blue eyes, and he put his face against hers, his hands tightening on her.

'Oh, Alisa,' he breathed against her skin. 'This is so foolish and you know it. It is a mad attraction that should never have happened. You don't even like me.'

When she murmured in protest he turned her face to his and ran his lips softly over hers, keeping tight control, not letting any emotion grow. It was gentle, as if he was consoling a child, but it was so sweet that tears came into Alisa's eyes. He brushed them away and sat her back, starting the car, saying nothing more.

Silence stretched between them as they drove on through the vast estate that was home to Luc, and he suddenly asked, 'How old are you, Alisa?'

'Twenty-four, nearly twenty-five. I—I told you that I went off for two years before I took up my place at university.'

'So now you are this great age,' he said quietly, his lips twisting in amusement. 'I am thirty-seven.' He grunted irritably. 'I am supposed to have reached the age of cold common sense.'

'You're very capable,' Alisa managed quietly, and he shot her a lightning glance of exasperation.

'Capable of what?' he growled. 'I am not quite as cold-blooded as you thought at first—not when I look at you.'

'We—we should speak about something else,' she said shakily, and he gave the same irritated growl.

'Think of a subject. If you can force your mind away from the subject that is occupying both our thoughts I will be very surprised.'

'Why don't you just send me back—let me go home?' she asked rather desperately.

He was silent for a long time and then he said, 'You are not well enough, and in any case, I cannot. I am not even sure that I can go away while you are in the house. We will have to see what sort of determination I can summon up. When I hand you over to my mother you will be much more safe.'

'She may not like me,' Alisa pointed out, and he smiled at her uneasiness.

'She will like you. Why should she not? You are one of her own race.'

'So are you. At least, you're half like her.'

'I am like my father,' Luc stated flatly. 'I do not even look like my mother. I am Bolivian. My mother never ceased to be English.'

'Does she ever want to—to go back?'

Luc shrugged and gave her a slight smile, turning his head to glance at her.

'I have never been sure of that. I have asked her in the past and her answer has always been the same. She loves my father.' He stared ahead, his eyes narrowed against the sun. 'I expect she does, but I must confess that I have never understood why. He is hard, unbending. Women are strange. They have the ability to make sacrifices that few men would make.'

It was disquieting, and left Alisa even more sure that she did not want to meet Luc's father.

He said nothing else. The car swept out of the long drive and they were at the house—the most fabulous house that Alisa had ever seen.

There was nothing European about it. It was a South American house, white and glittering in the sunlight, with cool balconies and high, curved arches that led inside. There were balconies, too, at the high windows of the bedrooms, and everything was nestling under a red-tiled roof.

Steps led down into a semi-tropical garden with lush green lawns and banks of brilliant flowers, and Alisa was stunned. She had not really thought about the kind of house she would see, but this was beyond her expectations. It was lovely, dream-like, and she told Luc fervently as he stopped the car and turned to her.

'It's wonderful!' she breathed, and he gave her a smile that lit up his dark face.

'It is comfortable,' he agreed. 'Come inside and meet my mother. She has probably been here for hours. This is a great excitement for her.'

Alisa had never felt so nervous. She was very much aware that she was stepping into a situation where she did not understand the people involved at all. She felt close to Luc. She wanted to be with him and admitted it, but she did not understand him. Now she was about to meet a woman who might not even be happy with her own life.

CHAPTER NINE

THE sound of her own feet on the cool tiles of the hall as they went inside seemed to be very loud, and she was finding it difficult to walk easily after so long in the car. Luc's hand came to her arm, the warmth cupping her elbow, helping her, and she gave him a glance of gratitude, ridiculously pleased when he smiled down at her. It gave her the courage to face the tall, slender woman who came out of one of the rooms to meet them.

She was very obviously English, in spite of her long years in Bolivia. Her face beautiful, her hair grey and smoothly coiffured, and she looked at her son with amused affection.

'Well, I'm here, Luc, as ordered,' she remarked, and he went forward to kiss her cheek.

'Thank you, *Madrecita*. You are an angel.' He turned and introduced Alisa. 'Here she is,' he said quietly. 'You will make her better, yes?'

'With pleasure.' The woman came and shook Alisa's hand. 'You're a very beautiful girl, Señorita Fenton. Very delicately beautiful,' she added, and Luc intervened, his eyes flaring over Alisa as the colour rose in her face.

'Her name is Alisa and she is almost a doctor. She is also tough, or so she insists.' He sounded quietly amused and his mother shot him a look of gentle reproof.

'You are embarrassing the poor girl, Luc. Come along, Alisa, I'll show you to your room. You look as if you need a rest. Don't let my powerful son tease you. When he has nothing better to do, he amuses himself by goading.'

Alisa knew that already, and as she glanced at Luc he grinned at her and shrugged, turning away as his mother led her up a long, curved staircase. He looked almost light-hearted and she had never seen that before. The look altered his whole face. At that moment he seemed to be more approachable than he had been since she had known him. She could hear him giving quiet orders to someone, and they had not even reached the upper floors before a maid brought up Alisa's one and only suitcase.

The maid was brightly dressed, an Indian, and she made a curious little bobbing gesture to Alisa as she darted inside a room and placed the suitcase on the floor. It was the room she was to occupy, and Alisa entered it with some misgivings. Once settled here she was stuck. It would somehow be an admission that she was prepared to stay, and even the sight of the beautiful room, the long windows open to the balcony, did not entirely drive away her doubts.

'Have a rest now, Alisa,' Luc's mother said as she simply stood and looked round the room rather anxiously. 'You look pale and tired. Luc told me about your dreadful accident and I'm sure it will be some time before you feel really well again.'

'Señora Sanchez—' Alisa began in agitation, but to her surprise, a gentle hand touched her arm and Luc's mother smiled at her in a very understanding way.

'Elizabeth,' she corrected. 'Let's not be formal—and don't worry. Whatever you need, Luc will get. He is very grieved about your accident and he wants you to get better. He told me you are uneasy about staying here. Don't be. I'm looking forward to getting to know you. Rest, Alisa. I will see to it that you're called for dinner.'

She smiled and left, and there was nothing for it but to have the prescribed rest. In any case, Alisa knew that she needed it. She was not as well as she had thought, and she took off her sandals and dress and slid beneath the cool sheets at once, her eyes beginning to close as soon as her head touched the soft pillows.

She was too tired to worry any more and the room was peaceful, the slight breeze blowing the curtains. Outside she could hear birds singing. It would be wonderful to live in a house like this. The whole place was like paradise. It was such a contrast to everything she had thought about Luc. To her he had been a powerful being who had controlled her days since she had met him. Now she had discovered another side to him, a more gentle side, and this house somehow emphasised it.

She opened her eyes sleepily as the door opened quietly, and Luc stood watching her, a slight frown on his face.

'You are all right?' he asked. 'My mother told me that you looked ill.'

'Just tired,' Alisa assured him, and he walked slowly across to her until he was standing looking down into her pale face.

'You are the doctor,' he acknowledged. 'You know if you are ill. The only anxiety I have is that you will not tell me if you feel worse.'

'I'll tell you.' Alisa managed to smile up at him, although her eyes were slowly closing, and he looked back at her for a second, his dark eyes roaming over her face.

'Then I will take that as a promise,' he warned. It was almost the old, threatening tone, and Alisa's eyes were closed but she smiled, a touch of mischief on her face. She was almost stunned into wakefulness when he added in a soft murmur, 'Go to sleep, *pequeña*. You are quite safe here.'

It was a sort of endearment, she mused as she fell into an exhausted sleep. She had the feeling that Luc had decided she was a child or something very like it. And all because she had fallen and banged her head.

'I'm tough as boots,' she insisted to herself, knowing that Luc had gone.

He had not gone but he said nothing at all. Instead he watched her with dark unfathomable eyes that had softened with amusement when he heard her muttered declaration.

It was easy to settle in at Luc's house. It was soothing, with the feeling that there was no other world—a sort of Shangrila below the snow-capped heights of the Andes. Each day was slow and calm, and Alisa was getting on very well with Luc's mother. By now, after all the years she had been married, Elizabeth Sanchez was more Bolivian than English, and she even had a slight accent, but there was no mistaking her enjoyment of Alisa's company.

Luc was not there. He had left the day after she had arrived and although she could not pretend that she was glad, she knew that it was for the best. He was being wise, removing temptation, and she wondered if she would even see him before she left. There was no mention of her departure, and Alisa was loath to bring up the subject. It seemed ungrateful to worry Luc's mother, and as Luc was not there the matter had to be left.

Dresses had arrived two days after she had come, and when she had protested in embarrassment Luc's mother had laughed and told her that Luc had ordered them in La Paz and had had them delivered. He had guessed the size but they were a perfect fit, and in spite of her uneasiness about them, Alisa was secretly delighted. There was swimwear too, and each day she swam in the pool behind the house. It was good for her leg and very relaxing. She gained a golden tan and her hair was burnished to a pale gold by the sun's rays.

'You look well,' Elizabeth Sanchez concluded one afternoon, standing by the pool and smiling down at Alisa as she floated lazily in the water. 'Luc will be pleased to see it.'

'Is he coming back?' Alisa asked, instantly excited.

'I would imagine so. He rings almost daily to find out about you. In any case, you are his guest. It's time he was here—entertaining you, taking you out.'

'Oh, I'm not that sort of guest,' Alisa assured her quickly. 'I'm just here to get well and then I'll be on my way home.'

'Home,' Luc's mother reminisced, sitting down in a poolside chair as Alisa climbed out and slid into a towelling robe. 'For a long time I used to speak of England as home. Now Bolivia is my home. I don't even dream of England. Sometimes I almost forget how to speak my native tongue.'

Alisa wanted to ask if she was happy, but it would have been impertinent. She did not know Luc's mother well enough to delve into her happiness.

'Luc will bring you to our house in La Paz,' Elizabeth Sanchez continued. 'It will help to brighten things for you and you can meet his father.'

Alisa hoped not. She felt very uneasy about meeting Luc's father. The things Luc had said to her about him had left a lingering impression of a near-aristocratic dictator, and she was not at all sure how she would react to any haughty declarations.

'I'm ready to go home,' she pointed out. 'I can't just stay here. When Luc comes I'll mention it.'

'I like having you here,' Luc's mother assured her. 'But I would not like to think that you felt unable to leave.'

'I've got a place in a hospital in England,' Alisa reminded her. 'I have to be there soon. I'll never really be a doctor if I don't take up my place there and get down to some work.'

It was the perfect excuse to leave, and she knew that she should go very soon. This idyllic situation could not continue, and while she stayed in Bolivia she was not going to be able to put Luc out of her mind. She slid back into the pool as Elizabeth left, and she was still there, floating dreamily on the water, when Luc arrived.

She didn't hear him come. The pool was at the other side of the house and she didn't even hear his footsteps as he approached. The first she knew of him being there was when she opened her eyes and found him looking down at her, his dark eyes roaming over her figure. It brought her out of her dreamy state and she stood up, her hands twisting the water out of her hair.

'I didn't expect to see you,' she began, but Luc didn't even smile.

'I want to talk to you,' he said, an aloof look on his face. 'Get out of the pool.'

He tossed her a towel as she climbed out and she drew it round her protectively, looking at him with a certain amount of foreboding. She knew his expressions well and he was not pleased.

'According to my mother,' he stated coldly, 'you wish to go back to England.'

'It's time I went,' Alisa pointed out nervously. 'I can't stay here forever, and I've got to get on with my training.'

'It is not the end of your holiday yet,' he reminded her sharply. 'You have some weeks left.'

'I haven't,' Alisa corrected. 'I'm not going back to university. I'm going into a hospital and I should be there next week. I'll lose my place.'

'It is not the only hospital in the world,' he snapped impatiently. 'You can go somewhere else.'

'I don't want to! Luc—!' Alisa began, and he stepped forward and clasped her against him, ignoring her wet state.

'I don't want you to go!' he told her fiercely, and Alisa looked at him in bewilderment.

'But you said it was not sensible. You told me you would be staying away. You've never even been here...'

'I have wanted to be here,' he muttered, tightening her against him. 'Finally I gave in. I had to see you.'

'You're getting wet,' Alisa pointed out shakily, and he looked down at the way his shirt was already soaking from the water from her bikini, his eyes lingering on the tempting swell of her breasts beneath the wet top.

'I am getting more than wet. I am getting desperate,' he said thickly. His fingers trailed across the swell of her breasts, sliding inside the top of her bikini bra, seeking the cool skin.

'Luc!' She gasped his name and his lips found hers, silencing her shaken protest. His hand pulled her fingers to his chest and held them there before he slipped a few buttons and drew her shaking hand against the smooth, strong muscles. 'Touch me,' he breathed against her lips. 'Touch me as you did that night in the mountains, but this time know what you are doing, mean it!'

It was too much to resist, and Alisa's arm wound round his neck, her fingers sliding into the thick darkness of his hair. Her other hand moved delicately over his chest, a light, butterfly caress that brought a growl of pleasure to his lips.

'Alisa!' he groaned, urging her further against him, ignoring the wetness that was invading his clothes. He sank with her to the canopied swing, its back and top concealing them from any eyes at the windows of the house, and Alisa was unable even to think of anything but being close to him and feeling this bliss.

Her bikini top fell to the floor under the searching impatience of his fingers.

'Your mother...!' she warned weakly, her head flung back in a wild torrent of feeling that raced through her, and his tongue moved to her neck in its urgent quest.

'*Dios*!' he groaned. 'I don't care. I just want you in my arms. I want to devour you.'

She was curled against him, her arms around his neck, and Luc was kissing her passionately. She forgot the proximity of other people and Luc seemed to have forgotten too. His hand was tight in her hair, forcing her head back as his lips roamed over her face, but then he seemed to take a hold on his wandering senses and gave a long sigh, looking down at her.

'Now you know that I am mad,' he said unevenly. 'You also know why I can't let you go.' He suddenly smiled at her, his lips twisting ruefully. 'You have moved into my soul, *encantadora*. I promised myself that it would never happen to me, but I did not know I would meet an English girl who was almost a doctor and tough as boots.'

'What shall I do?' Alisa asked helplessly, unable to move away, and he stood and put her on her feet, his hands moving caressingly over her bare shoulders.

'Want me,' he ordered softly. 'Stay with me.'

Alisa's eyes searched his face. She did want him and he knew it, but how could she stay? He didn't love her. It was just passion—something she had never felt before. He was thirty-seven, experienced, wealthy beyond her most wild imaginings, and his handsome face was so different from anyone she had ever seen. It was aloof, even though now his high cheekbones were tinged with the colour of his tempestuous desire for her. His eyes were still darkly mysterious, his thoughts veiled and secret.

Luc would never give everything of himself even if she knew him for the rest of her life. And then the rest of her life would not be possible, because his desire would fade and she would be lost here, stranded in a foreign land without love.

He was watching her intently, his dark eyes unwavering, prying into her thoughts, and Alisa reached for the towelling robe in order to give herself time to look away from him and avoid any answer.

'I will get changed,' he said quietly. 'Come inside and have tea. My mother still keeps her old customs, as you have probably found out.' He turned away and Alisa found her voice.

'When are you leaving?' she asked, and he spun around to look at her levelly.

'I am not. The Sanchez problems can take care of themselves for a while. I have a pressing problem of my own. If I leave you will escape, hurry back to England and some miserable hospital.'

'Luc, please!' Alisa begged. 'You can't keep me here.'

'I can't keep you if you wish to leave,' he agreed sombrely, and then he walked off, going into the house and leaving her staring after him.

If only there was more time—more time to get to know him. But maybe you never knew anyone enough. Maybe there never was enough time. If she left now she would always wonder how Luc felt, and she would never forget him.

Alisa gave a shaken sigh and then trailed after him into the house. By now she had no limp. She was better, and she knew deep down that she should go home. She was not sure, though, if she had the courage to leave Luc. Her planned career did not now seem to be so important. She had been excited about it before she came to Bolivia, but she had not known what excitement really was.

She looked up at the mountains that she could see from her bedroom, the snowy peaks glistening in the sunlight. She had found excitement there and she had found beauty there—and she had found Luc, a man from another world who could draw her to him with a smile and one word from that dark voice. Alisa shivered and went for a shower, her mind in a turmoil again.

'We are going to La Paz tomorrow,' Elizabeth said at dinner that night. 'Luc is taking us. It is only a few hours away. You will be able to go to the shops and see the city. You will also be able to stay at my house and meet Luc's father.'

The very idea terrified Alisa and she looked up quickly, her eyes finding Luc's. He had warned her about his father and now he was deliberately taking her into the den of that particular lion. And she couldn't refuse either. She was trapped. Elizabeth Sanchez was proud to be able to offer her hospitality, and Luc was looking at her with a sort of bland satisfaction.

'Thank you,' she said uneasily. 'It will be very nice.'

'Will it?' Luc asked in amusement when they were alone for a while. 'You are actually looking forward to meeting my father?'

'I don't have a lot of choice,' Alisa muttered. 'What did you expect me to say? Not likely? I've heard about him? Your mother seems delighted.'

'She likes you,' he pointed out wryly. 'I think she intends that you should meet her friends.'

'Why?' Alisa asked desperately. 'There's not a lot of point in it. I'll never meet them again.'

'You have decided, then?' he asked quietly. 'You are leaving me?'

'Oh, Luc! You were the one who said how impossible this was, how dangerous and out of the question. You were the one who said it was the mountains.'

'But it is not, is it?' He got up to pour himself a drink and turned to look at her steadily. 'We are here under normal circumstances and I still feel the same. So do you,' he added implacably.

'It's not normal circumstances. It's—it's out of my world, outside my experience.'

'It is my world,' Luc stated, looking into her eyes. 'I want you in it. I want to marry you.'

Alisa stood slowly on shaking legs, almost unable to believe her own ears. She had never expected him to say anything like that, and now that he had thoughts raced through her mind with too much speed for her to capture them.

'Why?' she whispered, and he put his drink down and came across to take her hand in his.

'Because I cannot let you go,' he confessed quietly. 'I would always be searching for you, always be remembering. Does it matter that we are different in so many ways? Does it matter that we have known each other for so little time? One day we will know each other, we will be comfortable together.' He cupped her face in strong hands and looked at her deeply. 'I will take care of you, look after you. When we go to La Paz, I will tell my father.'

Alisa was bewildered. He had not asked her. He had announced it firmly, and she didn't know whether to laugh or cry. Marriage was something she had not really thought about, but on the few occasions when it had slipped into her mind she had first thought of love, and Luc had never even considered that.

* * *

Next day, they could see La Paz as they made a spectacular descent from the mountain pass. It was the first time that Alisa had actually looked at it, because her arrival in Bolivia had been too tinged with anxiety to leave her more than a few minutes to spare for the sight. It lay below them, filling the bowl of a vast, rugged canyon, climbing steeply up the canyon walls. The snow-capped triple peak of a mountain towered over it and she sat forward beside Luc, wanting to look at everything at once.

'It is not London,' Luc murmured, never taking his eyes from the dangerous road, 'but you will find it interesting—and at night it glitters like the stars in the sky.'

He could see that she was fascinated and he could also sense her nervousness. Her slender hands clenched together and he frowned as he noticed it. She was dreading meeting his father and he knew it. Her ready tongue would be of little use to her. There was nothing he could say at that moment. His mother was sitting in the back of the car.

He reached out and took her hand, placing it firmly against the warmth of his thigh. He could feel the shock that ran through her at this intimate, protective gesture, but his lips curved in a smile when she did not move away.

The house was in a very wealthy area. It was built in the manner of old Spain—imposing, with wrought-iron balconies at the upper windows, intricately carved stonework and a double flight of steps to the front door. Long windows looked out over the garden and Alisa felt a renewal of anxiety as she saw it. This was where she would meet Luc's father, and there was no getting out of it.

It was quiet inside, with a vast staircase leading off the wide hall. After the sunlit airiness of Luc's house Alisa found it oppressive, but it was clearly the house of a wealthy family. She tried to get back her old attitude of nonchalance but failed miserably. The whole atmosphere was intimidating.

The man who came into the hall to meet them was intimidating too, in a way that Luc had never been. With Luc she had felt antagonism, a resentment of his power, but this man was very different. It was like seeing a grandee from the Spain of hundreds of years ago, and Alisa had no idea how to react to him.

He was tall, grey-haired and so autocratic in his bearing that she simply stood by Luc and stared, her inclination to turn and fly into Luc's arms almost too strong to be denied. Because this man did not approve of her at all. He had known that she was coming, known how Luc had protected her, and he did not like the turn of events.

'Señorita Fenton,' he acknowledged politely, with no sign of a smile. 'I have met your uncle, the professor. You are very welcome.'

She wanted to shake her head and tell him that she was not one bit fooled by the cool courtesy, but all she could do was manage a slight smile and remove her hand as speedily as possible when he took it in his. All the time he was speaking, greeting his son and wife, the dark eyes were inspecting Alisa, and she could almost be sure that he knew that Luc had bought her dress. Polite disapproval was written all over his face.

Dinner was an event—formal and lengthy—and afterwards Alisa longed to go to bed and escape. Luc had things to discuss with his father and she hoped that it was all business, because if he did what he had threatened and told Señor Sanchez about his plans for marriage she was sure she would be asked to leave immediately.

When Luc brought up her small case and walked into her room later she was on the edge of screaming.

'You must go,' she told him in agitation. 'You can't walk in here. If he should come up here and find—!'

'Steady, *pequeña*,' Luc warned laughingly. 'What has become of the girl who is tough and fights all the time?' He moved over to her, and before she could dodge away he had her in his arms. 'Like you, I am a guest here, and I will behave decorously, but it is many years since my father was able to either frighten or influence me.' He looked down into her anxious face, his hands roaming soothingly over her back. 'He is not quite as bad as he seems. It is just that he has this constant desire to dominate. He does not disapprove of you as a person—remember that he married an English girl himself. I am the focus of his disapproval.'

'He seemed to be aiming it all at me,' Alisa pointed out, and he bent his head, dropping a quick kiss on her lips.

'He was summing you up. He does not yet know how you fit into my life, but he will know soon enough because I intend to tell him.'

'Please don't.' Alisa pulled away and then turned to face him. 'I'm going home, Luc. I'm going back to England to take up my life again.' She sighed and looked away from the tension on his dark face. 'I feel as if I've been away for years. I've almost forgotten it. I must go back.'

'You cannot,' Luc said steadily. 'You will not be able to forget me. You want me. You need me.'

'I don't!' She turned away, walking to the window, but before she reached it Luc was behind her, his arms circling her waist, pulling her back against him with a movement so fierce that she felt the breath leave her body.

'You *do* need me!' he insisted harshly. 'Tell me that you need me!'

'I don't.' She pulled uselessly to get away but he merely tightened his hold until she gasped his name in a pleading voice.

'Don't fight me!' He turned her in his arms and tilted her face, seeing the drenched blue of her eyes, and his expression softened as his lips trailed over her cheeks. 'I never meant to hurt you,' he breathed against her skin. 'Why do you fight me, Alisa? Why do you deny everything that is between us?'

His hands were moving over her, his fingers probing the warmth of her waist, and Alisa felt her body melting, becoming fluid; her eyelids became heavy and he watched her, watched the remaining tears make their slow progress down her cheeks.

He would not let her look away, his hand holding her face up, his eyes never leaving hers, and Alisa took a shaken breath. She was trapped by his eyes, trapped by her own response to him. More tears flooded down her cheeks and she lifted her mouth to his in mute surrender.

'You belong to me,' he said softly. 'Do not make it so painful.' His palms spanned her waist and then moved up over the thin material of her dress. His eyes moved sensuously over her breasts before his hands covered their fullness. 'I will take you into heaven,' he whispered against her lips. 'I will carry your mind over the snow-capped mountains. You will forget England when you are in my arms.'

Alisa moaned against his lips. She already forgot everything even when he only looked at her, and when he touched her she was not really in the world at all.

'Adorata.' The warmth of his breath filled her mouth, and her heartbeats quickened when his tongue slowly invaded the moist darkness. Her own tongue met his secretly, tentatively, and as he felt her instinctively sexual response he captured her lips more forcefully, his hands moulding her to him until she had no doubt about his desire for her.

When she was shaking in his arms, her breathing painful and uneven, he drew back and looked down at her with sensuously possessive eyes.

'Now I can go,' he said quietly. 'Now it is safe to leave you—although I would rather stay.' He touched her face gently. 'Go to bed, Alisa. Tomorrow I will take you out, but soon we must go home. I want you to myself and in this house there is no privacy, nowhere to go where we can be alone.' He ran his fingers through his hair, muttering as he turned away, 'I sometimes wish we were back in the mountains, just you and I.'

So did Alisa. Things had been simple there, and she had been in possession of her own mind. Now she felt that she had given a commitment without one word being spoken and that Luc was about to make it official.

She went to bed, but it was a long time before sleep overtook her.

She knew that she was planning to change her life, to give up all she had worked for. There was no fooling herself. Luc was right. She did need him. And if this longing to see him, longing to feel his touch, to hear the sound of his voice and share his laughter was love, then she loved him too. When she admitted that she felt a wonderful peace, and sleep stole over her softly and easily.

Next day it was impossible to keep the knowledge out of her eyes, and Luc noticed it as soon as she came to breakfast. This time the formality did not bother her at all, and when Luc had settled her in her chair she smiled at everyone as she said good morning. Luc's gaze never left her face, and there was a light behind his eyes that altered his whole expression. Looking at him now it was incredible to believe that he had ever been harsh and domineering.

His father eyed Alisa thoughtfully, but there was nothing on his face to tell her that Luc had spoken to him about her. It was very apparent, too, that Elizabeth Sanchez knew nothing, because she was utterly normal—the only normal person present at the meal.

Alisa felt a twinge of alarm that she could not stifle, but she didn't have the chance to let it develop because Luc took her out almost at once, and the rest of the day was theirs. They roamed around the city and had lunch at the best hotel, and Luc's hand never left hers as they walked. She had never been in love before. It made her shy, light-headed, and Luc treated her with bewildering gentleness, his eyes smiling into hers every time she looked at him.

The roads were steep and after a while she was tired, but before they turned back to his mother's house Luc had bought Alisa a fine alpaca sweater with ancient Inca designs knitted into it and, best of all, a golden chain with a small replica of the Cat God she had found in the mountains.

'To remind you always,' he said quietly as he fastened it round her neck. She shivered at the touch of his fingers against her skin and his arm came round her waist as they turned to head back to the house. He knew exactly how she felt, and there was a burning satisfaction in his eyes.

There was another guest for dinner, and as soon as Luc saw her his face hardened. He shot a look at his father that would have killed a lesser man, but there were the usual polite courtesies and Alisa was also introduced.

'Señorita Fenton is recovering from an accident in the mountains,' Jorge Sanchez said as he presented the woman to Alisa. 'Her uncle is famous. He is Professor William Fenton.'

He didn't add that Alisa was staying with Luc, and after one look at the beautiful Spanish face Alisa's heart sank.

'Señorita Cristina Fuentes,' he introduced, adding with a great deal of satisfaction, 'Cristina is Spanish. Her family have been here for no more than ten years. Her father has property close to our own.'

Meaning that they were wealthy, acceptable, and that Señorita Fuentes was not some impoverished medical student who just happened to have a famous uncle. It had been smoothly said, but after one glance at Luc's furious face Alisa knew that he, too, had taken the subtly made point.

Alisa also knew that this woman was no casual visitor here. Cristina Fuentes knew Luc well, and after seeing her hand on his arm in a very familiar way, Alisa just wanted to walk out and fly back home. This was to have been Luc's future, and now she understood why his father had eyed her with such disapproval.

'Alisa is staying at Luc's house,' Elizabeth Sanchez said firmly during dinner. Cristina had spoken Spanish to Luc throughout the meal, but at this announcement all conversation stopped.

'Alone?' Cristina Fuentes asked, in a suitably shocked voice.

'So far my mother has been there,' Luc intervened coldly. 'I had to be away and it was not suitable to leave Alisa there alone. However,' he added quietly, 'I am back now.'

'I—I'll be very willing to go back with you to your house, Luc,' Elizabeth said rapidly, evidently unnerved by the growing storm of anger that her earlier words had unleashed. Luc looked thunderous and his father was white with rage.

'It will not be necessary, *Madrecita*,' Luc informed her with a tight smile. 'Tomorrow Alisa and I will leave. In any case, we must fly to England to see her uncle. She has also some personal business to attend to. Do not worry,' he added when his mother looked flustered and embarrassed, 'we are quite grown up. We do not need a chaperon. This is not medieval Spain.'

CHAPTER TEN

IT WAS only courtesy that kept the meal going, because there were few words after that, and Alisa wanted to run from the room. Everyone was shocked, and she knew that Luc had spoken deliberately to strike a blow at his father. She also knew without being told that Cristina Fuentes had been invited here tonight so that her own unsuitability could be impressed upon Luc.

Later she was sure of it. She was barely upstairs before Luc stormed into his father's study and began immediately. The language was Spanish and too swift for her to follow, but she knew that there was a furious argument going on. She got into bed, pulling the sheets over her head. She didn't want to hear, didn't want to know. She had stepped into an alien culture where brides were chosen, it seemed. Luc was supposed to marry Cristina Fuentes, and he did not like being pushed into anything.

She had been there and willing. She was nothing more than a fierce protest from Luc, a show of his determination to be master of his own fate. He did not love Cristina Fuentes enough to marry her and he was being pushed into it. Alisa knew that he didn't love her either. It was desire and her ready acceptance of it. Now she felt like a victim. Some foolish girl who had blundered into a scenario she knew nothing about.

There was a tap on her door, and when she sat up and put on the lamp Alisa saw Luc's mother standing there looking very shaken.

'Come in,' she said, instantly sorry about all the trouble.

Elizabeth Sanchez was sorry too, and she came inside and closed the door.

'You must be very upset by tonight's events,' she began anxiously. 'Luc and Jorge can be so unfeeling and overwhelming, and I opened up the whole thing by my thoughtless remark about you staying with Luc.'

'But your husband knew,' Alisa pointed out. 'He also knew you were there.'

'Yes, but you heard what Luc made of it,' Elizabeth reminded her. 'It was because my husband insisted upon inviting Cristina for dinner. He did not tell Luc and I had no way of warning him because you were out all day.'

'It doesn't matter,' Alisa assured her softly. 'Families quarrel. Don't worry on my account.'

'I wish this was all over,' Luc's mother sighed, sitting at the side of the bed and looking miserable. 'If they were not so alike! Tell Luc to do something and he will be sure to take the opposite view. His father is exactly like that, and he cannot seem to keep out of Luc's affairs. Not in this matter, at least. Luc is thirty-seven, and according to Jorge he should be married. If there had been no interference he would have married Cristina long ago. I just know it. He will not be pushed into things, though, and I can only sympathise with him. There is a touch of ancient protocol about my husband.'

'It will sort itself out when I've gone,' Alisa said soothingly as Luc's mother left.

And she was going. In the morning she would leave for England. Most of her things were at Luc's house but there was nothing she would miss. He had bought her the dresses and she could not consider taking them. She was here in La Paz and getting to the airport would be simple. A taxi would get her there, and she knew that Luc's father would be all too pleased to take her there himself if need be. Luc would not be pushed into things and neither would she. Loving him was one thing, being a pawn in some power game was another. She would not marry Luc and have Cristina Fuentes over her shoulder for the rest of her days. It was time to go.

It was dark when Alisa walked out of the hospital and set off along the road to her flat. She had been at the hospital a month now, and she was getting used to it, but today had been a long day and it was tiring.

Coming here had been a wrench—leaving her uncle's house, leaving the university and all her friends—but she was settled in now. As settled as she was going to be. She sighed, her fingers finding the golden chain that hung around her neck beneath the collar of her white shirt. She pulled the small Cat God into her hand and held it in her palm for a few seconds. It was comforting. It reminded her of the mountains, the soaring peaks, the blazing sun and the cold nights round the fire with the unearthly music of the Andes rising into a dark, star-filled sky.

It reminded her of Luc, and she let it fall back into its secret place between her breasts. She didn't need to be reminded about Luc. She would never forget him. He was always in her mind; the sound of his dark voice haunted her days, his strong arms haunted her nights.

Escaping from him had been so easy. She had come down the morning after that dreadful evening expecting to have a confrontation, but he had not been there. Some crisis had taken him away to one of the mines. His father had gone with him and his mother had told her that they expected to be back in the afternoon. That was when Alisa had announced her intention of leaving immediately, and Elizabeth Sanchez had not been fooled.

'You love my son, don't you Alisa?' she had asked quietly, and there had been no way to deny it.

'Yes. I love Luc, but I'm going all the same,' she said. 'I've stepped into a situation I don't understand. I'm in a land where I don't belong. I'm going home.'

'If he loves you he'll follow,' Elizabeth warned, looking at her steadily, but Alisa shook her head, smiling slightly.

'He won't. In any case, he doesn't love me.'

'That's what I thought long ago,' Luc's mother assured her. 'I went back to England too, but Jorge followed me and here I am.'

'Do you regret it?' Alisa felt able to ask, and Elizabeth Sanchez smiled happily.

'Never for one moment. He's arrogant, domineering and annoying—but I love him and he loves me. I would never have been happy without him.'

Alisa had made her escape, partly with Luc's mother's help, and she had flown back home, taken up her place at the hospital and told nobody at all about Luc, about her heartache. And he had not come. She had not really expected it. He knew she was going to be a doctor.

She smiled to herself wistfully. That was how she was addressed now—Dr Fenton—and it seemed all wrong. Somewhere along the line she had lost her drive to succeed; somewhere along the line she had changed her heart and her mind. It was difficult to concentrate, to go on studying and working the long hours, because the commitment was no longer there. She wanted to be with Luc.

She reached up as she walked, tiredly pulling the pins out of her hair, letting the long golden plait fall silkily down her back. Even that reminded her of Luc and the garden of the hotel. With everything she did or said she seemed to be wilfully remembering him, torturing herself. Since she had come back to England she didn't feel alive any more. With Luc she had seemed to be wildly alive all the time.

She was walking past the small park now and her flat was just around the corner. It was quiet, the road empty, but she had made this journey many times. Very often she was late coming back and it had never worried her.

Suddenly Alisa's skin tensed. She realised that just behind a car was steadily keeping pace with her. It had been there for some time and she had only just noticed. Until this moment she had been wrapped in her own dreams, but now she came back to reality with a rush.

It was dark, late, only the lights of the streetlamps keeping total blackness away. This was a good area but it was stupid to be too confident, stupid to take risks. She quickened her pace, her eyes on the corner, and almost sank down with relief when the car suddenly accelerated, turning the corner and moving out of sight.

When it had gone the silence seemed to be heavy with menace, but once round the corner she would actually be able to see her flat and she hurried on. In future she would take greater care. Her heart was still pounding with alarm, the burst of fear still gripping her mind.

She turned the corner and gave a scream of fright when she found the car waiting, parked by the kerb. A tall, dark figure was standing beside it and Alisa turned to run, but she was not nearly fast enough. Two arms wrapped around her waist and she was pulled relentlessly against a strong body.

She began to kick out frantically, but her wild struggles stopped as a dark voice said mockingly, 'I thought you were tough as boots, *señorita*. You are not even cautious. Once again you are walking at night when you should be safely in bed.'

'Luc!' She just whispered his name but he heard her, and his arms tightened possessively.

'Who else?' he enquired softly against her ear. 'Are you going to fight me, *pequeña*, or are you going to take me to this flat of yours and explain your very bad behaviour?'

He turned her slowly in his arms until she was looking up into his face, her gaze captured by dark, flashing eyes, and she was shaking so much with fright and shock that she just rested her face against his jacket, allowing him to hold her as her trembling hands clutched at his shirt for comfort. He folded her close, his hand stroking her hair, and it was such bliss that Alisa didn't move at all.

'*Bueno*!' he said quietly after a few seconds. 'Now we will go. Get into the car. I will park at your front door and see that you do not escape a second time. You are certainly not capable of being out alone.'

At that moment Alisa could only agree, and she kept her trembling lips tightly closed and did exactly as he ordered. They were only a few yards from the door to her flat, but Luc did not mean to let her out of his sight. He was right beside her as she found her key and it was Luc who took it from her and unlocked the door, checking that it was securely locked behind them as they went inside.

He said nothing at all and Alisa moved nervously, avoiding his eyes, taking off her coat and walking through to put it in the bedroom. She had no idea what he was going to say to her, no way of knowing why he had come here or even how he had found her.

He followed her to the bedroom door, watching every move she made, and then he took off his jacket and tossed it to a chair, loosening his tie and sitting down to stare up at her as she came back into the tiny sitting room.

'Now,' he said sternly, 'you may explain your peculiar behaviour.'

'There's nothing to explain,' Alisa began uneasily. 'I just came back home. I live in England, Luc. There was a place waiting for me at the hospital and...'

'You call this odd place home?' He glanced disparagingly around the small flat, ignoring everything else she had said. 'It is no more than a shoe box.'

'I can't afford a bigger place!' Alisa pointed out crossly, annoyed with herself for even answering this autocratic interrogation and even more annoyed with herself for wanting to fall into his arms. 'I'm still poor. It's clean,' she added mutinously.

'So are most refrigerators,' he murmured drily, 'but I would not expect to find you curled up in one. However, the matter of your way of living can be left for the moment. I want an explanation of your behaviour. My father is astonished that my future wife fled so speedily.'

'You're going to marry Cristina Fuentes,' Alisa said miserably. 'If your father hadn't insisted you would have married her years ago. The only reason you haven't married her is because you like to annoy him. It's no use denying it because your mother told me.' She looked at him with pain-filled eyes. 'I'm not a fool, Luc. I knew what was happening the moment I saw her.'

'Did you, *encantadora*?' Luc murmured. He stood and came slowly towards her, following when she backed away. She felt the hardness of the wall behind her and there was nowhere else to go. She stood looking trapped, and Luc's eyes softened with amusement at her predicament. 'There are few opportunities for escape in a shoe box,' he pointed out lazily, and when Alisa darted sideways he simply collected her and held her in the loose circle of his arms.

'Please let me go, Luc,' she pleaded. 'I know you're probably in England to see Uncle Bill and this is just a brief visit to goad me.'

'I have seen the professor,' he confessed steadily. 'How else was I to know where you were? I came to get you and could not find you. Now that I have found you I will take you back. I know where home is for you and it is not here in this dismal place. It is in Bolivia with me.'

Before she could speak his head bent and his mouth opened possessively over hers, taking her breath away. His arms tightened and she was no longer loosely held; she was securely trapped as Luc always trapped her.

'I won't be second choice, Luc,' Alisa cried, tearing her lips away from his. 'I won't be used as a means to get at your father.'

She began to struggle wildly, and Luc simply lifted her and walked to the chair he had left. He sat down and held her securely on his lap, trapping her arms as she fought him still.

'You are not being used as a means to defeat my father,' he said fiercely. 'Listen to me, you crazy girl!' He cupped her face in his hands and made her look at him. 'I am not and never was about to marry Cristina. She is a friend only, as your Douglas is a friend to you.

You do not love him; you would not consider marrying him. He is a friend, as you told me. That is what Cristina is to me. We have never had any desire whatever to marry or even to kiss each other.'

Alisa's struggles subsided, but she still looked at him warily and he shook his head in exasperation.

'How I am going to cope with you for the rest of my life, I do not know,' he said softly. 'I know, however, that I cannot manage without you. I cannot leave England if you do not come with me. I will simply follow you around, and the Sanchez business affairs can manage without me or collapse entirely.'

Alisa went on looking up at him, but now her eyes were wide and blue, the shadows beginning to go from them.

'I love you, *querida*,' Luc said softly. 'There is no need to fight. You have already won.'

'I don't want to win, Luc,' she said tremulously. 'I'll live wherever you like.'

'Because?' he insisted, tilting her face to his.

'Because I love you too,' she whispered, and that was all he waited to hear. His lips closed over hers and she was wrapped in warm arms that cradled her close. Her arms wound around his neck and she stopped pretending. She was safe, comfortable, enclosed in the destiny she had felt when she had first seen him.

'I didn't think you would come,' she whispered as he tilted her face and placed heated kisses over her cheeks and neck. 'I missed you all the time.'

'My father suggested that I give you time to think,' he murmured huskily. 'He gave my mother time to think when she ran away from him and came back to England. Unfortunately I do not have his patience. A month seemed like a year. I was with you in the mountains, seeing you every day. Then you were in my house and in my arms. Being without you was too painful. I needed you too much to wait any longer.'

'I needed you too,' Alisa whispered. 'I've hated every minute without you.'

'So you will come back with me?' His hand cupped her face and he looked down into her eyes. 'You will marry me and let me take you home?'

'Oh, yes, Luc!' She looked up at him ardently and for a second he stared down at her, his face tightening with desire. His hands skimmed her body lightly, but there was so much passion in his touch that Alisa trembled and lowered her lashes, her cheeks flushing with soft colour.

'You sleep in that little room?' he asked in a low voice, his lips against hers.

'Yes,' she said tremulously, and he trailed his lips over her hot cheeks, his tongue finding the corner of her mouth, teasing its way along her lower lip with a sensuous slowness that made her heart pound wildly.

'Will you sleep there with me—now?' he asked softly, and all Alisa could do was moan in agreement as her lips parted at the insistent invasion of his tongue. He crushed her against him, kissing her into a deep, drugged submission, his hands slowly slipping the buttons of her blouse and finding her breasts.

'*Querida*! You're so beautiful,' he breathed. He looked down at her, his eyes feasting on her silken skin, and then his hands drew her trembling fingers to his chest. 'Touch me, Alisa,' he groaned. 'Show me how much you need me.'

She did need him, and her hands were unsteady as she unfastened his shirt and ran her fingers delicately over the smooth muscles, teasing him until he gave a low growl of impatience and lifted her into his arms, standing and making for the small bedroom that was softly lit by lamps.

Luc slid her to the floor and began to undress her slowly. When they had been by the pool at his house he had seen almost all of her, but this was different. Here, nobody was likely to interrupt them. Here, she was totally committed to Luc, and as she looked up into the smouldering darkness of his eyes Alisa could see how much Luc was involved with his own emotions.

He had forgotten that this was new to her, even if he had ever known it. A trembling unease grew in her stomach, the feeling mixing with the pulsating awareness that was already there, and when he had removed her covering she stood with her head bowed, feeling vulnerable and slightly lost, aware as she had never been of Luc's masculine power.

'Luc,' she whispered desperately, and he tilted her chin with strong fingers.

'I know,' he said softly. 'You are a virgin and you are afraid of the unknown, afraid of pain.' He slid out of his shirt and drew her against him, his hands running soothingly over her back. 'One moment of pain and we belong to each other, *querida*. I will not forget that you are afraid.' His dark eyes burned into hers. 'I will not devour you. I have you for the rest of my life.'

'I want to—to belong to you,' Alisa said shakily. 'Sometimes I've felt as if I already do. That night in the mountains when...'

With a low, vehement groan, Luc tilted her face and claimed her mouth, his kiss powerful and endless until she was shaking in his arms, her body urgently seeking his.

'*Dios*!' he muttered hoarsely. 'I cannot stand here with your naked body wound around mine and simply kiss you. I have been feeling desperate for far too long.'

He swung her off her feet and placed her on the bed, and Alisa moved fretfully against the coolness of the covers as he swiftly undressed. When he joined her she felt another burst of fear as she felt the strength and inevitability of the lean, muscular body that moved over her. She stiffened and Luc looked down into her eyes, his hand tracing her face.

'*Tranquilo,*' he murmured. 'I love you, *querida*. One moment and you belong to me.'

He did not demand that moment immediately. Instead his hands slid over her warm, silken skin, his lips teasing at hers, biting gently along her lower lip, his tongue tracing the shape. His fingers caressed her breasts, bringing everything inside her to singing life, and Alisa twisted urgently against him as his lips explored her body sensuously.

His kisses and the slow movement of his body seduced her until she was gasping in his arms, fighting to be closer, and when he moved over her more urgently, his hands running convulsively over her hips, she found her legs parting of their own accord, her body rising naturally to meet his, as he possessed her swiftly.

'Now there is just you and I, and nothing to keep us apart, *pequeña*,' he told her gently.

Alisa looked up at him with wondering eyes. She knew so many things, but nothing had prepared her for the feelings that filled her now. As she relaxed his dark eyes held hers, and then his lips covered her own, fiercely possessive. She moaned weakly, her body shaken by his driving possession as everything left her mind and she slid into a velvet-dark world of sensuality.

She could dimly hear her own cries mingling with Luc's deeper sounds of satisfaction, and then she fell over the brink of pleasure into a spinning world of light, stars flashing in her mind as Luc groaned her name and collapsed against her.

'Querida,' he said thickly after a moment. 'Let me hold you close.'

It was only then that Alisa realised that she was still gripping him tightly, her legs wound around him, her arms locked round his neck. Colour flooded into her face and Luc laughed down at her as he gently extricated himself and rolled away, pulling her into his arms and settling her head against his shoulder.

'You tricked me,' she complained shakily, burying her face against him. 'You didn't tell me when.'

'You will know when in future,' he assured her with lazy amusement, tightening his arms possessively. 'I seem to have waited a long time,' he added with a deep sigh. 'It was difficult, *querida*, not to take you in my arms that first night in the garden of the hotel. You looked very beautiful—so intriguing and so satisfyingly scared of me.'

'You brute!' Alisa pummelled his chest and he caught her hand in his, smiling to himself as he remembered.

'I could not quite resist touching you.'

'It was disgraceful,' Alisa pronounced, and he grinned at her, his fingers trailing over her hot face.

'De acuerdo,' he agreed. 'It had to last for quite a while, though. I did not get another chance to hold you until you came creeping out of your tent in the moonlight. You were very lucky, my darling, that I did not take you into my tent for the rest of the night. The inclination was there and your resistance was low.'

'I didn't even know you liked me,' Alisa protested. 'I thought it was a sort of punishment.'

'It was,' he agreed wryly. 'I was punishing myself. Sleeping for the rest of the night was impossible.'

'I understood that you didn't like women,' Alisa sighed, lifting her face to be kissed as he tightened her to him.

'My father has been pushing them at me for some considerable time,' Luc muttered. 'Considering that I am as stubborn as he is, the whole thing has been tiresome. I had no intention of being burdened with one when I went into the mountains—until I saw you,' he added seductively. 'Then I was in a fix. How to take you with me and not appear to be in a state of surrender? Luckily José García was not well enough to go. It was a magnificent excuse.'

'I refused to go,' Alisa pointed out triumphantly, and he sighed and looked down at her.

'I know. You were infuriating. Fortunately your anxiety about your uncle was enough to force you into acceptance. It was hard to tell him that the expedition was off. His face was so tragic. If you had not agreed, of course, I would have made the trip without a doctor.'

'What?' Alisa sat up and looked down at him with stormy eyes. 'You said that—'

'I can manage the odd bit of medical assistance,' he assured her, his dark eyes laughing into hers. 'It was a matter of whose nerve would break first. Your nerve broke, *adorata*. You did not like to see the professor so gloomy.'

'You're very tricky!' Alisa pointed out heatedly, her face flushing wildly as he bent his head and began to kiss her breasts.

'It was necessary. I wanted you,' he murmured huskily. He looked up at her, his smile fading. 'I did not know how much I needed you until you fell. I thought you were dead.' He pulled her down to him, gripping her fiercely. 'In that moment I knew that it was more than desire. I didn't care whether or not I fell myself. I only knew that I wanted to be with you for the rest of my life.'

Alisa lifted her head and kissed him, and it was much later that she lay sleepily against him and asked about his father.

'He doesn't like me,' she announced mournfully. 'There'll be trouble.'

'There will be no trouble, *querida*,' Luc stated firmly. 'My father was impressed. After I had laid down the law a little and told him that I would marry you, he became most enthusiastic. He drove over to the mine with me so that we could talk. Imagine his astonishment when we returned and found that the bride had flown. My mother was very annoyed with him, and he retired to his study in a bemused state.' Luc suddenly laughed and hugged her close. 'He was finally very pleased. He says that history is repeating itself. My mother ran away too.'

'She told me,' Alisa muttered. 'He chased after her.'

'And I chased after you,' Luc said with a good deal of satisfaction. 'We will be married here, in England. My parents will fly over for the wedding. Your friend Douglas can be a guest. So can Cristina.'

'Cristina?' Alisa asked, frowning at him ferociously. 'I'm not putting up with—'

'Cristina will be on her way back to Spain,' Luc informed her with amused patience. 'She is also in a state of revolt. Her family moved to Bolivia when she was twenty, and it was not her idea of paradise because she left her childhood sweetheart behind. She is going back to marry him.'

'Oh,' Alisa murmured, greatly relieved.

'You will be leaving your hospital behind,' Luc said after a few minutes. He tilted her face and looked deeply into her eyes. 'Will you be willing to do that? Is it something that you will finally come to resent?'

Alisa smiled at him, dispelling his worries.

'It's something I've thought about. Since I've been back, my enthusiasm has faded. I was never exactly sure what I wanted to do.' She sighed and settled comfortably in his arms. 'That's why I went travelling before university. I always wanted to do what Uncle Bill did, but I wasn't sure if I would be any good at it. I suppose I drifted into medicine because of Africa. It's not exactly a good reason for doing it. I'll have to find something else to do.'

'You can have children,' Luc said softly, turning her in his arms and hovering over her. 'It is something we can do together.'

'I could go on some of the digs,' Alisa said dreamily a good while later.

'If we are not climbing and if I think it is safe for you,' he agreed. His hand came to touch the little golden Cat God that hung between her breasts. 'I can get a helicopter up to the lake,' he mused seductively. 'This time we can have our own tent. You would agree to that, *querida*?'

'If I can have warm water each day,' Alisa laughed, and his eyes darkened as he smiled down at her.

'Warm water each morning and warm desire each night,' he promised.

* * *

Three months later, the tents were once again set up by the lake, and Alisa sat with Luc beside the fire as they ate the evening meal.

'The same old team,' she said with a grin, glancing at her uncle, who was studying the day's finds with Douglas and Jeff.

A gleaming helicopter stood on the flat land close by, and Chano was very proud to have been flown here in it.

'It will be your last trip for some time,' Luc warned. 'I will not let you take any risks. When the baby arrives you will be too busy. This was not a good idea even now.'

'As a doctor, I know exactly how I feel,' Alisa reminded him pertly, and he slanted an intense look at her before putting his arm round her and drawing her closer.

'You were only ever a learning doctor. Now you are an ex-doctor. You have other responsibilities, Señora Sanchez. Besides, I do not always come on these trips. You imagine you would be allowed to come without me?'

'I would never want to,' Alisa whispered, looking up into his eyes. 'I hate it when you're not there.'

'Am I ever far from you?' Luc asked softly, and she shook her head, nestling against him, happiness brimming over inside.

'Do you think Chano knows I'm pregnant?' she whispered after a minute, when Chano, as usual, had cast a beaming smile in her direction.

'I'm never sure what these people know,' Luc assured her with a laugh. 'They are an old people. They see much and say little.'

'He might just make a good nursemaid,' Alisa mused. 'He certainly fusses enough. Uncle Bill is fussing too.

He wants Betsy to come when I'm ready for having the baby. It's ridiculous.'

'He is probably paying you back for the years of fussing you have forced on him, *querida*,' Luc laughed. 'They may all come—providing that we can be alone for most of the day and all of the night.' He suddenly looked up to where the setting sun was gilding the mountain-tops. 'Look, *mi amor*! *El cóndor*.'

It was gliding above the mountain, silhouetted against the golden glow, its magnificent wings spread wide, and they watched it until it was out of sight.

'The spirit of the Andes,' Luc murmured as it disappeared.

'Perhaps,' Alisa said softly, her hand in his. 'To me, though, the spirit of this place is you. This is where I found you; this is where I lost my heart. I think about your strength and your kindness. I look up and see your strong face, your black hair and your beautiful eyes, and I know I wouldn't mind living up here in a tent with you for the rest of my life.'

'I love you, Alisa,' Luc said deeply, looking into her eyes, and she saw all the love in the world there, everything to give her courage and happiness. A flare of passion crossed Luc's dark face and his hand tightened convulsively.

'It is night,' he said thickly. 'It cannot come soon enough for me. That is when I have you to myself. I think, my darling, that very soon your uncle will have to come here without us and take his chances.'

'I know,' Alisa agreed softly. 'I don't want to share you either. Maybe one day we won't feel like this?' She looked at him wistfully, and Luc brought her to her feet and smiled down at her with adoration in his eyes.

'When the sun no longer shines and the mountains are gone,' he agreed. 'Until then, we will feel the same.'

She could never doubt the promise in the dark eyes, and they went hand in hand to stand by the others and look over the treasures. Inside they had a greater treasure—a love that would go on forever and never be lost.

MILLS & BOON®

Three women make a pact to stay single, but one by one they fall, seduced by the power of love!

Don't miss Penny Jordan's exciting new miniseries—The Brides Bouquet coming to you in the new Mills & Boon Presents line in September 1996.

Look out for:

Woman to Wed? in September
Best Man to Wed? in October
Too Wise to Wed? in January '97

Available from WH Smith, John Menzies, Volume One, Forbuoys, Martins, Woolworths, Tesco, Asda, Safeway and other paperback stockists.